Asher

(Wolves of Winter's Edge, Book 3)

T. S. JOYCE

Asher

ISBN-13: 978-1542555609
ISBN-10: 1542555604
Copyright © 2017, T. S. Joyce
First electronic publication: January 2017

T. S. Joyce
www. tsjoyce.com

All Rights Are Reserved. No part of this book may be used or reproduced in any manner whatsoever without written permission, except in the case of brief quotations embodied in critical articles and reviews. The unauthorized reproduction or distribution of this copyrighted work is illegal. No part of this book may be scanned, uploaded or distributed via the Internet or any other means, electronic or print, without the author's permission.

NOTE FROM THE AUTHOR:

This book is a work of fiction. The names, characters, places, and incidents are products of the writer's imagination or have been used fictitiously and are not to be construed as real. Any resemblance to persons, living or dead, actual events, locale or organizations is entirely coincidental. The author does not have any control over and does not assume any responsibility for third-party websites or their content.

Published in the United States of America

First digital publication: January 2017
First print publication: January 2017

Editing: Corinne DeMaagd
Cover Photography: Furious Fotog
Cover Model: Tyler Halligan

DEDICATION

For the best teammate I could've asked for.
Ty, this one's for you.
#TnT

ACKNOWLEDGMENTS

I couldn't write these books without some amazing people behind me. A huge thanks to Corinne DeMaagd, for helping me to polish my books, and for being an amazing and supportive friend. Looking back on our journey here, it makes me smile so big. You are an incredible teammate, C! Thanks to Golden Czermak of Furious Fotog for this shot of Dylan for the cover, and for being my hilarious backpack-buddy.

TnT. Y'all probably already know who I'm about to thank just from those three letters, but the other half of my signing team is Tyler Halligan, and whooo we have had some adventures. And more than that, outside of the chaos and fun of the events, he is one hell of an inspiring person.

To my cubs, who put up with so much to share me with these characters, my heart is yours.
You keep thanking me for working so hard for you, but that always blows my mind. You are worth every ounce of effort, no thanks needed.
You are the amazing ones.

And last but never least, thank you, awesome reader. You have done more for me and my stories than I can even explain on this teeny page. You found my books, and ran with them, and every share, review, and comment makes release days so incredibly special to me.

1010 is magic and so are you.

PROLOGUE

Asher was leaking the black fog again.

He stumbled over a tree root in his desperation to get farther away from the house before the darkness took him. His body was vibrating. Inky, dark tendrils spread from his hands, reaching for anything living, and then roiling clouds of black brought the energy back into his body. Every plant the fog touched died. He was killing the forest around him. He sniffed and blinked back tears. Even at seven years old, he knew he wasn't supposed to be like this. He tossed a look over his shoulder to make sure Gentry and Roman weren't following him. They would get hurt if they were around him when he was like this. When he was The Taker.

All that followed him was a trail of dead, dry, gray plants. The forest was alive and green except what he'd killed. A bird chirped on a low-hanging branch. It was black with brown eyes. Pretty, shiny feathers, but it was a dumb bird. Not afraid. Didn't it see The Taker in him? The fog was reaching, stretching, concentrating on the bird.

"Fly away!" Asher yelled, but it was too late. The bird flapped its wings to escape, but Asher already had him. He was already feeding on him. The bird's head drooped, and it fell off the branch and turned dead and gray just like the plants. At least the bird was bigger and had filled Asher's hunger. The fog seeped back into his skin and, horrified, Asher picked up the bird's body. A tear streaked down his cheek. He'd killed it. He'd never hurt an animal before, but he'd killed this creature that hadn't done anything wrong.

He squatted down and began frantically digging in the dirt. He had to bury it. Bury it before the spirit haunted him like the other ghosts standing around watching him. He had to bury it before Roman and Gentry saw it. Before Dad saw it and realized how bad he was. Before Mom saw it and cried again. She cried every time she saw The Taker in him.

Asher laid the little body into the grave he'd scooped and covered it with rich, black earth as fast as he could. While he was patting it down, from behind him his mom murmured, "It's okay, Asher."

He whimpered and spun, riddled with guilt. "I didn't mean to."

Mom wrapped him up in a hug, like he wasn't bad or scary.

"I don't want to hurt you," he cried. But he clutched onto her shirt because he wanted her to keep hugging him anyway.

"You can't hurt someone like me," she whispered.

"Why not?"

Mom knelt in front of him and gripped his shoulders. Her black eyes searched his face, and her black hair whipped around her shoulders. There were tears in her eyes. "Because, Asher, my boy, I'm like you."

"You are?"

She gave him a small smile and nodded her head. "I've figured out a way to make this easier on you."

"How?"

"I'm going to take your powers into myself, but

there will be a downside."

"What's a downside?"

"It means we'll both have to make a sacrifice to make you like the other boys."

Asher didn't understand, so he wiped his cheeks with his knuckles and shook his head.

"Asher, I'm going to give you a wolf, like your father has. I have to make you and your brothers stronger to fight what you are. The wolf will give you strength to fight the power you were born with. Does that make sense?"

No. Not at all. He'd seen Dad's wolf but couldn't imagine being one. Asher didn't want to disappoint Mom though, so he shrugged and said, "I guess. Will it hurt you?"

Her smile was so sad. "Not much. It'll hurt how it has to, but I would do anything for you, my boy. Anything. Do you want to be rid of it?

"Of The Taker?"

"Is that what you call it?"

Asher nodded solemnly. "I hurt things, and then I feel stronger."

Mom's face crumpled, and she stared off into the woods for a minute, swallowing over and over. "I'm going to fix The Taker in you, Asher. There's one last thing, though."

"What?" he whispered.

"When it's all done, you and your brothers aren't going to remember me." She inhaled sharply like the words hurt badly, and now twin tears streaked down her cheeks.

Asher reached forward and touched one. It absorbed into his finger, and he felt the energy from her sadness. "I hate The Taker, but I don't want to forget you, Mom. Not ever."

Mom pulled Asher in close and hugged him tight. And then she stood and held out her hand for him to take. "Come on, my Asher Boy. We have work to do."

ONE

Ashlyn Jenkins narrowed her eyes at the trio of cabins surrounding her. The parking lot was empty except for her own car, and no lights were on in any of the cabins despite the late hour. Snow blew across the concrete in sheets, and outside the warmth of her rental car, the wind howled. Hunter Cove Inn looked like a ghost town.

Her best friend Blaire had lost her damn mind. That was the only thing that explained her going on a vacation Ashlyn had planned, and then never coming home. Oh, she called occasionally and had even sent her a picture of the three men she now lived with. Giants, the lot of them. Albeit sexy giants, but Ashlyn had sat through this horror movie before and could see it plain as day. Her best friend was playing Goldilocks and the Three Murderers.

"Eeny meeny miney mo, catch a serial killer by the toe. If he hollers, stab him a lot," she muttered, gripping the handle of the pocket knife she'd bought at the general store in town. "Eeny meeny miney mo." She'd never been a very good poet.

Ashlyn chugged the last of her strawberries-and-cream Frappuccino and tossed the cup to the floorboard like a badass, then thought better of dripping on the rental, picked it up, set it carefully back in the cup holder, and shoved the door open with the heel of her snow boot. "Let's fuckin' do this."

She marched right up to the biggest cabin, the one that said 1010 on the house number, and took the porch stairs two at a time. She puffed her chest up and reared her hand back to blast her knuckles on the wooden door.

"I wouldn't," a man said.

Startled nearly to death, Ashlyn jumped back from the door and clutched her chest.

The man was one of the beasts from the picture Blaire had sent. The big one. He stood—and stood and stood—so that Ashlyn's head rolled back to take in his massive size. He wore a black T-shirt as if the cold didn't bother him and black sweats. He held a black cup of something hot in his hand and wore a black winter hat over what looked like blond hair. His eyes were a vivid, light blue, and his jaw was chiseled and dusted with short, blond facial hair. He was sexy as fuck if she ignored the deep frown on his face.

Ashlyn gulped. "I'm here to rescue my friend."

The man canted his head in a way that reminded her of a curious animal. His eyes, however, didn't look curious at all. They looked angry. "What the fuck are you wearing?"

Taken aback, Ashlyn looked down at her bright pink jacket and matching pink ski pants. Was he referring to her leopard print snow boots? Those were just as hot as the rest of her fitted outfit.

"Rude," she said curtly. "What the fuck are you wearing, *Johnny Cash*?" The man's mouth fell open and his frown deepened, but before he could respond, she held up her hand primly. "No matter. Where's Blaire? We have a flight to catch."

The man snorted. "Blaire isn't getting on any flight, so why don't you take your blinding outfit and your attitude back to your wildly-inappropriate car for this weather and leave."

"It's a smart car! I get like four hundred miles to the gallon!"

"It's a matchbox car, and the tires are nearly bald. Try not to die on your way to the airport," he growled as he strode past her.

Fury blasted through her as he walked by, and losing her mind completely, she grabbed the belt of his pants and held on as he dragged her a few feet across the icy porch.

"No," he ground out. "No touching."

Nausea rolled through her stomach, and suddenly her hands hurt so bad, she lost her grip.

His eyes looked lighter when he turned around. God, he had a lot of muscles poking out of his shirt. And tattoos. Was she going to barf in front of him? Ashlyn wrapped her arms around her stomach and swayed on her feet. Maybe it was the ten packages of airplane biscotti cookies she'd stolen from the flight attendant's cart when she wasn't looking. Perhaps karma was now giving her food poisoning.

"Sorry," the man muttered.

"Sorry for what?" she asked. "I probably shouldn't have grabbed your...butt."

"No, you shouldn't have. Blaire's not here. She's in town with the others. Won't be back until late."

He turned and opened his door, then let himself into the dark room. He really wasn't going to invite her in! Ashlyn dashed into the door opening, and then sighed in relief when she made it all the way in before the sexy giant got it closed. Victory.

"What are you doing?" the man asked in an exasperated tone.

"Whoo, it's dark in here. I can't see anything."

"I can. Now get out." The door opened again.

"Polite decline. Do you have hot chocolate? I'm cold."

"Do you have no sense of self-preservation at all?" he asked.

"I don't know what that means, but I'm super thirsty for something hot and sweet, and if Blaire is going to take forever in town, I want to wait inside here, where it's warm, instead of my"—she deepened her voice to make fun of him—"*wildly inappropriate car*."

The man let off a long, harsh sigh that tapered into a weird sound that was slightly scary. He slammed the door so hard, she jumped. The hollow sound of his boots against the wood floors told her he was walking away. Seriously? He really wasn't going to turn on the lights?

"It's still dark in here."

"I like the dark. If you have a problem with it, fix it."

"God, you're so rude," she muttered as she felt along the wall for a switch.

"I'm rude? You barged in here and demanded hot chocolate."

"Because I could tell you weren't going to offer!"

"Because I didn't invite you in!"

"My name is Ashlyn," she introduced herself angrily.

No answer, but she could make out the tinkling sound of a ceramic mug.

Her fingers fumbled around for a minute before they slid onto a light switch. Score. She flipped it on and winced at the bright illumination.

There was a stone hearth built with rocks of all different shapes and sizes, but it wasn't against a wall. There were stone steps leading up behind it to a hallway, probably where the bedrooms of the house were. There were scuffed wood floors and log walls and a cute kitchen off the living area. On the back wall were a pair of French doors that showed the snowy landscape of the backyard.

"Whoa," she whispered in awe, stepping carefully into the big room.

"You're standing in a ghost," the man said blandly from where he was pouring hot coffee into a mug.

What a weird combination of words. Ashlyn looked down and around her, but nope. No ghost.

"Look, can you just move three feet to the left," the man gritted out.

"God, you're weird."

"Well, at least I'm not wearing all pink. You're hurting my eyes."

"Maybe it wouldn't hurt your eyes if you turned on a damn light every once in a while and added some color to your own wardrobe. Why are you so grumpy? Are you like one of those mountain hermits who hates people?"

"Yes," he deadpanned. And then he made his way to her—his boots echoing against the floorboards too loudly—and shoved the half-full mug of steaming coffee at her.

"This isn't hot chocolate."

"And you're a beggar. Don't be a chooser, too. I don't have hot chocolate. I have coffee. Black."

"Of course, it's black." She dragged her gaze down his monochromatic clothes and tried to look severe as she took the mug. "Thanks."

He gave her an empty smile. "My pleasure. I'm gonna call Blaire and hurry her up."

Ashlyn sipped the coffee and made a bitter face. "Good luck with that. She isn't answering her phone right now," she said as he pushed buttons on his phone. She'd called her a dozen times over the last couple days, but nothing.

He pulled it up to his ear and said, "Hey, you have a visitor, an annoying one... I don't know, Blaire, she's loud. And pushy. Ashlyn. Great, see you in a few."

Ashlyn made an offended noise. Blaire answered for him? But not for her supposed best friend? Sudden emotion prickled her eyes, but the man was staring at her now, and she didn't want him to see how slapped she felt. Blinking hard, she made her way to the kitchen and set the mug near the sink. "You can drink the rest of this," she said thickly. "I promise I don't have mouth herpes." As she walked past the man, she murmured, "It was kind of nice to meet you. Thanks for calling her."

Feeling utterly rejected, she made her way to the door and opened it.

"I'm Asher," the man said from behind her.

She turned and made an attempt to smile, but it came out a stupid lip tremble instead. Ashlyn swallowed hard and tried to make a joke. "Do you go by Ash for short, too? Because then we could be Ash and Ash."

"No." His tone had come out hard and cold, but at least his eyes had softened a little.

"Fantastic. It was super fun talking to you Ash*er*. Have a nice time in your precious dark." She flipped off the light switch just to piss him off and closed the door a little too hard behind her.

But when she made her way back to the car and got in, he still hadn't turned the light back on. She frowned at the shadowy house. What a sexy weirdo.

Maybe Asher really did like the darkness.

TWO

What the hell just happened?

Asher's heart was banging against his chest like some creature trying to escape the bars of his ribcage. His breath came too rapidly, and his hands tingled with the first phase of the Change. He clenched his fists and looked out the small peephole on his door to catch a glimpse of Ashlyn sauntering to her car, arms wrapped around herself like she was cold.

Pitiful, beautiful human. It was her color that made him release a long exhale. He could see everyone's color. Maybe it was their aura, he didn't know. He didn't give a shit what it was called. He only knew he could see things beyond this world, and

Ashlyn was a pure and vibrant blue, like a clear sky. Like summer after the rains. He'd never seen a color more beautiful than hers.

Which made no sense because she annoyed the shit out of him. She pestered, demanded, joked, and smiled too much. She would be an exhausting woman to keep occupied. One of those who had probably never sat still a moment in their life. An on-the-goer, where he liked to sit still in the shadows and observe. She was a creature of the light, and he was a creature of the darkest corners. The Taker in him would love to taste a woman whose color looked so pure, but the wolf in him snarled at the idea. Protective instincts? Did he have those? Maybe with Gentry and Roman, Blaire and Mila, but not with a stranger. Not with a human. Humans died too easily. He could swallow up her light and turn her into a gray, dead thing in minutes.

Movement caught his attention, and he slid a hate-filled glance to the ghost of Dad who was walking from the other side of the room toward him, worry in his eyes. "Stop," Asher commanded. And he did. Asher smiled. Dad probably hated that Asher could control him in the afterlife. Prick deserved to be controlled. He'd ruined Asher's life the day he kicked him out of the pack.

The other ghosts along the wall moved closer, shaking their heads, trying to tell him something he didn't care to listen to, so he flicked his fingers and banished them from the house. They disappeared in plumes of mahogany smoke. All but Dad, who lingered.

"She's important." Dad hadn't moved his lips, but his words rang clear as a bell through the house.

With a snarl, Asher banished him, too. Fucker knew better than to talk to him. He hadn't tried until now, and something about that made Asher angry. His first words should've been, "I'm sorry." They should've been, "I was wrong to kick you and Roman out of the pack, wrong to choose Gentry as my favored son, wrong for sending you straight to Hell." Not, "She's important."

Asher picked up a vase from the table by the door and chucked it at where Dad had stood. It shattered against the wall, but didn't make Asher feel any better. The darkness was still swallowing him up.

Outside sounded the soft rumble of Ashlyn's car starting up.

Blaire hadn't really answered the phone. She couldn't. She was out in the woods of Winter's Edge, running as a wolf with Gentry, Roman, and Mila. Asher had just pretended, and then instantly regretted it when he saw the hurt on Ashlyn's face. She must be one of Blaire's friends to show the slap of betrayal on her pretty face like that.

Pretty face, pretty color. Blue like her eyes. Chestnut-brown hair streaked with little honey-colored highlights. Side swept bangs covering one of her eyes. She had this direct way of looking at him that made him uncomfortable and excited all at once. It made him feel like she would see him and maybe he should hide. But it also made him want to step out of the shadows and into the light so she could tell what kind of monster he really was. He wanted to test her and see how fast she fled from him. Silly human wouldn't survive long if she had no instincts against barging into the lair of a beast. He snorted at the thought of her demanding hot chocolate in that harmless, sexy voice of hers. Pissed-off kitten demanding milk from a demon. A smile began to stretch his lips, but he stopped it. It was dangerous to be amused by that pretty little creature. Dangerous for her.

He was The Taker, and she would be The Giver, and he could ruin her life with the flick of his fingers.

She's important.

To Blaire maybe. Not to Asher. Nothing was important to him.

Lie, his inner wolf snarled.

Asher let off a long, low growl. Dark Wolf was overstepping boundaries. He was growing soft around Roman and Gentry. Around Blaire and Mila. He was connecting with living things in a way he shouldn't. Nothing survived him. Asher needed to leave soon, but first, he would bring in the wolves because the thought of Ashlyn waiting out in the car in the cold was something he suddenly couldn't stomach.

Disturbed by that inconvenient instinct, he opened the back door and jogged down the slick stairs, then knelt at the edge of the dark tree line. He could call them in with a howl. He could force their Changes and drag their unwilling bodies right to him in a matter of moments. Power like that drained him, though, and he had to be careful with The Taker. Especially with something so tempting sitting in the parking lot while blaring—Asher tilted his head and strained his ears—Backstreet Boys? She was singing every word, too. Nice voice, but she was punching out each word at the top of her lungs.

God, what a mess. A beautifully dangerous mess.

Asher knelt in the snow and touched the cold ground with the flats of his palms. Inhaling deeply, he rolled his eyes closed and searched for them. Ears straining, senses stretching, he was flying over the woods. The trees glowed blue, and the ghosts stood stock still, scattered among them. He followed trails and tracks, faster and faster until he could feel them close. Mila and Blaire were playing. White wolf. Gray wolf. Glowing, transparent like the ghosts, but they were still alive. He could feel them. They always made him hungry, but he would never hurt them. He would cut The Taker from his veins before he drained them. They were good. Angels in wolf forms. The girls had earned his fealty. The fealty of the biggest demon. Lucky them. Gentry and Roman were fighting fifty yards away from the girls. Ripping into each other, they were serious. Always serious. Wolves like Strikers needed blood and pain to stay steady. That was Mom's bloodline that had done that to them. The blood that sprayed the snow looked black from way up here above the trees.

Time to bring them home.

Home. The vision wavered as Asher frowned. Home was Hell, not these woods. He forced himself to cling to the vision harder, to focus, and then he dove toward the earth like a missile until he hit the snow and blasted into a cloud of black smoke.

Come back to 1010. Now.

Yeah, he'd given them an order. He used to be more careful, but fuck it all, they knew he was messed up. He'd let his façade slip too much in recent weeks. They knew he could order them around and control them like he was a real alpha. He wasn't, though. He was just king of the monsters.

Asher opened his eyes and smiled as a long howl lifted into the air. Gentry was pissed.

He stood and made his way through the woods, brushing his fingertips against tree after tree, pulling from their life-forces until he felt sated. One of the trees splintered at the lower trunk and fell immediately, crashing through the woods and landing on a smaller pine at an angle. Good. Firewood.

Dusting snow from his hands, Asher made his way in through the back door of 1010. Fuckin' house. Roman and Gentry had decided Asher needed to be the one to live here while he stayed in Rangeley. They said he needed whatever magic mojo Dad had been convinced this place had. He knew what it was, though. Gentry was trying to distance himself from Dad's memory by living with his mate Blaire in one of the smaller cabins instead of Dad's old house. And Roman knew the damn place was haunted by Dad's ghost and thought if he lived with Mila in the middle cabin, Dad would leave him alone. Sucker. Thanks to a boring afterlife, Dad had nothing better to do now than stand around and stare at them, Roman included. Gentry was so fucking lucky he didn't see ghosts. All he got from his lineage was a wolf that was separate from his human side. Boo-fuckin'-hoo.

Asher had a separate wolf, saw ghosts like Roman, had easy access to black magic, and had The Taker. His life revolved around trying not to kill everything in his path. But good for Gentry and Roman for shacking up with some great girls. Asher snarled and slammed the back door behind him. Why the hell was he envying them? It wasn't like he could ever have that. He couldn't have pretty things. Pretty things turned gray and ugly in his hands.

He could see everything inside the cabin. It wasn't a lie when he'd said he liked darkness. The shadows comforted him. It's where a creature like him belonged. He could see better in the dark, hear better, sense better. The light in the fridge was too damn bright as he pulled a beer from it, so he closed it fast and twisted the top off the bottle, dropped the cap to the counter, and took a long swig. He stared at the stupid *I love you beary much* magnet Roman had made for Dad in second grade. That was before Roman had realized he couldn't win Dad's affection unless he morphed into Gentry.

Annoyed, Asher ripped the magnet off the fridge and chucked it into the trash. This place sucked. Carefully, he lifted the blind on the front window. Ashlyn was rubbing her hands together, her shoulders hunched like she was cold. Her mittens were the same eye-scorching pink of her jacket and ski pants. Did the woman own anything that wasn't neon?

The blue of her aura was so wide it encased the entire car. She was still singing, but too soft for him to understand the words now.

The back door flew open and banked against the wall. "What the fuck, Asherhole!" Roman yelled.

He really hated that name.

Asher let the blind fall and turned slowly as Roman flicked on the light. The illumination hurt, but Asher composed his face as Roman hissed at him like a vampire. A naked vampire who apparently didn't give a shit about clothing himself in front of Mila and Blaire. He'd always been the potential nudist of the family.

Blaire and Mila were naked, too, but were at least covering themselves as they slunk up the stairs toward the bedroom where there were changes of clothes in the closet.

Gentry didn't bother with shaking him down. Nope, Gentry blurred to him and cracked Asher across the face with a closed fist. "I told you to stop forcing that stuff!" he yelled. "We aren't your pack, you prick! We're rogues and don't answer to an alpha, and you've been pulling that alpha shit way too much lately."

Asher didn't even fight back, just licked blood from his split lip and gave his middle brother an empty smile. "Blaire's friend is here."

"What?" Gentry asked.

"Ashlyn is here to take Blaire home." Asher strode by Gentry, slamming his shoulder as he passed. "Your mate, your problem. Get rid of the human before the Bone-Rippers figure out she's here."

"The Bone-Rippers won't hurt her. They aren't under Rhett anymore."

"Yeah?" Asher asked too loud, turning at the stairs. "Who are they under? Mila hasn't claimed her place yet. She hasn't even fucking told them she took alpha. You've got a pack of monster wolves that Rhett fucked up, all without any leadership, all human-haters. But sure, Blaire's friend is probably super-safe in Rangeley. It's a good risk to take."

Roman flipped him off, and without a thought to the consequences, Asher gave into his anger and snapped his fingers. Dad appeared right beside Roman in a plume of black smoke. Roman startled hard and then set his shocked gaze on Asher.

"Flip me off again and see what I can really do," Asher dared him.

Wide-eyed, Roman covered his dick, sidled away from Dad, who was staring at him, and then angled his face to expose his neck to Asher.

Not that he cared about Roman showing submission. Asher knew he was monster. Knew he was dominant. Didn't want it and didn't need the fealty of his brothers or anyone else in this world. It was just another stupid reminder that he was different.

He curled his lips back and gave Roman a hate-filled glare before he climbed the stairs behind the hearth two at a time and made his way into the bathroom. There were too many Striker brothers in too small a space. It made him want to kill things.

He turned on the light out of anger to punish himself. They had everything—mates… Well, they had mates, and that was everything, right? They had companions, and he was destined to walk this earth alone. The light flickered and buzzed as Asher stared at his blazing silver eyes in the mirror. And for a second, he imagined it. He imagined holding hands with a woman like Ashlyn—someone light and happy, who sang at the top of her lungs and wore bright colors.

His aura was black, and hers was blue, and a beauty and a beast did not a power couple make. Not when it would get the beauty killed.

Asher gripped the edge of the sink as the lights buzzed harder and one of the bulbs blew.

It wasn't fair.

"Asher, cut it out!" Blaire yelled through the bathroom door. "You're going to kill the power to the inn again!"

Fuck. Asher sighed and closed his eyes, loosened his grip on the sink, and thought about the way Ashlyn had demanded hot chocolate like she wasn't a fragile Red Riding Hood talking to the hungry wolf.

Blaire and Gentry would fix this, convince her to leave, and all would be well in Hunter Cove again.

Only the thought of her leaving did something strange and awful to his wolf, and the rest of the lights popped and showered him with sparks.

Downstairs, Roman yelled, "Seriously, Asher? God, you're such a boob-dick!"

Asher sighed and gritted his teeth, then shoved off the sink and yanked the door open. Blaire and Mila were feeling their way down the hallway toward the stairs, holding hands and looking all pitiful. They were wolves, and their vision would adjust soon, but in the meantime, he snuck past them quietly and jogged down the stairs to go mess with the fuse box.

He smelled her before he saw her. He turned around and ran right into the little pink-clad hellion. She cried out and scrunched up her face, her hands splayed on his chest. Asher froze. Her touch felt so fucking good. Heart hammering, breath coming in short pants, he whispered, "What are you doing in here?"

"I saw the lights go out."

She was looking up in his general direction, but couldn't see in the dark like him. God, she was pretty, her face all upturned like that, her hair cascading around her shoulders, lips pursed in confusion, delicate eyebrows arched. The others were talking low around them, but Asher couldn't make out a single word as he stood here, trapped under her soft hands. He pushed her hair back off her shoulder just because he could, just because he wanted to feel its softness.

Could he kiss her? Would she let him experiment? Would she let him touch his lips to hers if she knew how dangerous it was? He shouldn't, but he couldn't stop staring at her full bottom lip. He wanted to suck the lip gloss off it.

Slowly, he cupped her cheek and leaned forward, only to have a squealing Blaire rip Ashlyn out of his arms.

They were hugging now, but Ashlyn's searching gaze was still in his direction. She wore the cutest little frown he'd ever seen, as though she was as baffled as he felt right now.

What had possessed him to almost kiss her?

And what had possessed her to let him touch her cheek and not flinch away?

The lights came on, and the moment was ruined with him wincing. Probably best. His eyes would be light silver right now, and even though Ashlyn was talking to Blaire, her gaze was still on him.

Utterly confused by how urgently his wolf wanted to scrabble toward the strange beauty, he swallowed a growl and made his way out the back door as fast as he could. And only when he reached the woods, the cabin far behind him, did he turn around. The ghosts were gathering again, watching him stare after Ashlyn.

Little mystery all dolled up in pink and blue.

Pink and blue. Dark Asher, and she was a colorful siren that begged him to test his boundaries.

Dangerous creature.

Ignoring the ghosts around him, Asher pulled off his T-shirt and shucked his pants. He needed to do something with the energy that hummed through his body. His fingers tingled where he'd cupped her cheek. So warm and soft, and she'd trusted him to touch her in the dark.

His body wanted her. His head knew better.

The Dark Wolf exploded from his body and hit the snow on all fours.

Ashlyn was a delicate flower, brightly colored to attract, and he was the storm that would rip her to shreds.

He—Asher Striker, The Taker—was better off far away from such fragile beauty.

THREE

Asher had almost kissed her.

Right?

Ashlyn was trying to focus on her reunion with Blaire, but she was having trouble keeping her attention off the back door where Asher had disappeared.

"Ashlyn! Have you heard a word I've said?" Blaire asked.

Ashlyn blinked hard and dragged her gaze back to her best friend…who somehow looked completely different and exactly the same. Her hair was still the same copper-red, and she wore it in long beach waves, but her cheeks were rosier, and her eyes looked a couple shades lighter than she remembered.

There were other things, too, differences, but for the life of her, Ashlyn couldn't put her finger on what.

"You seem…" Ashlyn narrowed her eyes, searching for the right word.

Blaire's eyes flashed with worry. Just an instant of concern before she was smiling again. It was a plastered smile, though. "I seem happy?"

Ashlyn parted her lips to say "no," but yelped instead as Blaire dragged her over to a tall man with spiked-up dirty-blond hair and bright green eyes.

"Gentry, this is Ashlyn, my best friend. Ashlyn, this is…my Gentry."

My Gentry.

Blaire and Gentry were looking at each other so openly, so lovingly, Ashlyn clung a little more desperately to her hatred of him. Whatever was happening to Blaire here, it was bad. Gentry had stolen her friend away, kept her at this commune of giant—albeit sexy—brothers, and had made Blaire forget her entire life, including her best friend.

Maybe she was on drugs.

Ashlyn pulled Blaire's face toward her and spread her eyelids wider with her fingers, checking for pupil dilation.

Blaire swatted her hand and laughed. "Stop it, Ash."

"Remember that one time you ate that pot cookie, and then you went paranoid crazy for a day, and nobody could find you?" Ashlyn asked.

"I'm not on pot cookies!"

Ashlyn sniffed her for weed just in case, but she just smelled like vanilla, like always.

"Uuuh, nice to meet you," Gentry said, offering her his hand.

Ashlyn glared at it and crossed her arms over her chest. "I don't know what you've promised her, but this is all ridiculous." She waved her hand around the cabin. "Blaire has a good job—"

"Which I'm still working, just from here."

"—and a good life—"

"I was divorced with zero dates coming my way and an urge to buy, like, seventeen cats."

"—and the best friend ever, and she just packed up and moved. No! You didn't even pack up. You made me do it! You couldn't even come back to say goodbye and get your stuff? I had to pack up your big-ass house, and I had to talk to your stupid-face ex about his stupid record collection, and I've been falling apart at home, and you aren't there." Ashlyn hadn't meant for the last part to happen, the part where her words turned to a sob and her shoulders hunched. "And I miss you," she whispered through tightening vocal cords. "So, whatever is happening here, I want it to stop. People don't do this. Especially not safe, careful people like you, Blaire. They don't just go on vacation and never come back to their real life! They don't just leave their friends behind." God, she sounded pathetic, but there it was. All on the table so Blaire could see the error of her ways.

Blaire's green eyes rimmed with tears, and she hugged Ashlyn tight. She didn't say anything, only swayed with her while Ash fell to pieces and speckled the gray sweater Blaire wore with her tears.

"What do you want me to do?" Blaire asked.

"Come home. If you like this guy, great. Date him like a normal person."

"From a distance?"

"Yes, Blaire. Date him from your home town. Don't just change your whole life for a man! You did that for Matt, and look what happened."

"Gentry isn't Matt."

Ashlyn stomped her foot and shook out of the

hug. "You're so deep in this love-fest you can't see how unhealthy it is, Blaire! I got us plane tickets back home. Come back, at least tie up your loose ends, for God's sake! Clear your head and then decide if you want to be with this guy."

"This guy has a name," Gentry deadpanned.

"Where's the graham crackers?" a tall, muscle-bound bearded man called from the kitchen where he currently had his bare ass hanging out of the pantry as he shuffled through stuff on the shelves.

"Case in point," Ashlyn said, jamming a finger at the muscular rump of the stranger. "You haven't looked disturbed at all that there is a naked man looking for cookies right behind you."

The man snorted an offended sound and straightened, then leveled Ashlyn with a look. "Graham crackers are not cookies. Can you smear peanut butter and jelly on cookies? Hmm?"

"Yes."

He frowned like she'd stumped him. "Well, it wouldn't taste good."

"Roman, put some pants on," Gentry growled.

"For why?"

A dark-haired girl with a bright red headband

holding her bangs back snickered. And now Blaire was smiling, while Roman looked from face to face with his hands on his hips and his giant dick dangling there for all to see.

Roman inhaled deeply like he was going to say something profound. "Everyone has genitalia—"

"Nope!" the petite woman said, hooking her arm in Roman's and leading him toward the back door. "We're not going through the nudity-is-natural speech again. Goodnight everyone."

"Night, Mila," Blaire said with deep affection in her voice. "See you in the morning."

Ashlyn watched her best friend stare longingly after the couple that exited the house, and a sudden pang of jealously unfurled in her chest.

She'd been replaced.

Coming to Rangeley to retrieve Blaire wasn't supposed to be this painful. She'd imagined herself an eagle, swooping down to save her friend, but now Blaire had new friends, and she didn't seem to want rescue.

"You want to slumber party?" Blaire asked, turning to Ashlyn.

"In our cabin?" Gentry asked.

Blaire tossed him a frown, but he only shrugged. "It's small, and there's only the loveseat. Here would be better. Asher will be gone most of the night, and there is an extra bedroom. Win-win."

Ashlyn glared at the ignoramus. Of course, he would want her separated from Blaire so she couldn't remind her about her life outside of his clutches.

"I could sleep here with you," Blaire suggested. "It's a twin bed in the guest room, but we could squish."

"No. It's fine," Ashlyn gritted out with a forced smile. "I'll sleep here, and we can talk more in the morning. Over coffee and a bagel? There's a breakfast place I passed in town."

"Oh." Blaire frowned.

"What's wrong?"

"Well…it's just that Mila and I were going to do breakfast. You're welcome to come! We're going to Jack's at eight in the morning. I just don't want to cancel on her. She's been looking forward to some girl-time."

"Great," Ashlyn muttered, feeling like the third wheel on Blaire and Mila's stupid friend-date. "Eight o'clock."

"Ash," Blaire said, sympathy pooling in her eyes as she reached for her.

She squeezed Blaire's hand fast and then made her way to the door to avoid showing her friend how badly she was hurt by all this. "I have to get my bags," she announced.

"I'll carry them in," Gentry said from behind her.

"No, thank you!" she said too loud. He hunched his shoulders as if she'd hurt his ears. With an empty smile, she said at normal volume, "I appreciate the offer, but I don't need your help." *Ever, dick-weevil.*

Gentry threw his hands up in the air in surrender. "Suit yourself. It was really nice to meet you."

"Well, it was really weird meeting you." *Cult leader*. Ashlyn cleared her throat loudly and lifted her chin. "Good night."

"Ash…" Blaire murmured, pity tainting her name.

"I said good night!" Ashlyn turned and bustled onto the front porch and slammed the door too hard behind her.

Stupid Rangeley, and stupid sales lady who told her she looked good in the pink ski suit, and stupid Roman and his stupidly big dick, and stupid Mila-the-new-best-friend, and stupid Gentry for putting a spell on Blaire and ruining everything. And stupid her for coming here in the first place!

Blaire wasn't coming home. Not unless Ashlyn reminded her of everything she'd left behind. Not unless she reminded Blaire of what normal was, and that didn't include living in a nudist colony with three mountain men.

Disproportionately angry, Ashlyn stomped down the porch stairs toward her rental car. She slipped twice and barely caught herself on the black ice, and by the time she reached the passenger side of her car where she'd shoved all her luggage, she was crying. And true story, crying in frigid temperatures like this was miserable. Her tears were freezing on her cheeks.

She wrestled her pink luggage out of the tiny car, and immediately, a wheel popped off when she dropped it on the ground. The stupid little cylinder went rolling away like it was a professional escape artist. Ashlyn looked dejectedly after the wheel, urged on faster by the wind, and then shouldered her two duffle bags full of shoes and began dragging the suitcase across the ice.

Movement caught her attention on the edge of the

woods near the cabin, but when she scanned the trees, there was nothing there but shadows. Still, the fine hairs lifted on the back of her neck as she got the distinct feeling she was being watched. She forced her legs to move double time, nearly slipped again, and then bullied the broken suitcase up the porch stairs to the big cabin. Her noodle arms were shaking by the time she reached the front door, and Ashlyn swore to goodness she would try harder in yoga when she got back home. No more slacking off to watch the hottie who liked to do his perfect-form downward dog in the front row. Time to build up her own muscles because she would never turn into a lovesick, doe-eyed boy-chaser. Boy-chasers joined cults, apparently.

Ashlyn shouldered the door open and frowned at the empty living room. Someone had built a fire in the hearth, but the room was empty. "Hello?"

No answer. Clearly, everyone left through back doors around here. More weird shit, yay. The broken wheel was going to scuff the wood floors, so Ashlyn picked it up, cursed her need to overpack for a one-day trip, and wrestled the luggage up the stairs. First bedroom on the right looked like the guest room. The bed was made and the drawers empty. Blaire had been wrong about the twin bed, though. This was definitely a queen. Score.

She didn't bother unpacking. She was staying optimistic that Blaire would see the light, and they could leave by mid-afternoon tomorrow. Goals. That, Ashlyn could do. Set short-term goals, reach them, make more goals, reach them, repeat for infinity. That can-do attitude had gotten her far in life.

She readied for bed and felt watched again when she was brushing her teeth. She scanned the room behind her through the open bathroom door, but there was nothing there. Asher had put her on edge with his "you're standing in a ghost" comment. Creepy McCreeperson.

Creepy but hot. Asher was even hotter than Yoga Andrew. Asher would look glorious in some little tight tights in the downward dog position, mmmm. Ashlyn smiled to herself at her naughty thoughts, jumped into bed, bullied the covers, and fluffed the pillows until she had the perfect nest.

The room had an old-fashioned clapper light, so she clapped twice and grinned when the lights turned off.

Now she was in the dark, like Asher enjoyed. He'd almost kissed her earlier. She'd felt his hand on her cheek, his nearness, his intent. And when the lights had come on, he'd been close, his gaze focused on her lips as if he'd been able to see in the dark. There had been a split second when she saw his eyes before he pulled away. Pretty eyes. A really light, silvery blue.

It had been months since she'd been kissed, and she'd be lying if she said she hadn't wanted him to. How exciting to kiss a stranger who looked like Asher.

Asher and Ashlyn. Hmm. Maybe she would doodle their names together in her sketchbook tomorrow just for funsies. "Ash and Ash," she murmured into the darkness.

So grumpy, so mysterious, so sexy and utterly kissable. His hand had been gentle on her cheek. Ashlyn brushed her fingertips across her cheekbone to remember the feel and the warmth of him.

Too bad she was leaving tomorrow.

With a sigh, Ashlyn rolled onto her side and hugged a pillow.

If she wasn't on a rescue mission, Asher would've been fun to play with.

FOUR

Crouched down, head canted, Asher watched Ashlyn's sleeping form in the dark.

His Dark Wolf was hunting. The Taker was hunting. Asher couldn't stay away from her. The blue color around her, the scent of her shampoo, the shade of lip gloss she wore on her lips. Did he want to kiss her or consumer her? He didn't know yet, but there was this desperation in his middle to find out.

Earlier, he'd circled back to the inn and watched her cry as she took her luggage out of her car. He'd watched as she set down her blinding pink suitcase on the ice, only for the wheel to pop off and roll across the slick surface. He'd watched the defeat in her eyes as she tracked its progress across the icy asphalt. And then he'd watched fear consume her face as she'd listened to her instincts that she wasn't alone, and she froze right there in the middle of the blustery parking lot.

He'd seen that same fear a thousand times. It filled men's eyes when they got too close to him and recognized him as *other*. It filled mothers' eyes when they walked too near and had to hustle their children farther away because their protective instincts told them he was *monster*. But seeing it in Ashlyn's eyes bothered him in a way it hadn't ever before. If she saw him—*really* saw him—saw the black wolf with the silver eyes, she would run in fear.

But why the fuck did he care? She was a stranger.

Ash and Ash. He'd been sitting right outside her room when she'd uttered those words, his back against the wall while he'd listened to her get ready for bed. She'd put their names together. Well, at least she'd put nicknames together. No one called him Ash. He was Asher. Except when he and his brothers were kids, they'd called him Basher when they deserved to have their faces pummeled and he obliged them. Which had been often.

So, she was thinking of him, just like he was

thinking of her.

But then again…maybe he'd imagined it. Perhaps it was wishful thinking to want something beautiful to think of something dark like him.

He'd crept into her room as soon as her breathing slowed and he knew she was asleep, but something irritating pulled at his instincts. Something was happening outside. Asher stood from where he crouched near the door and strode silently for the window. He scanned the winter woods outside but didn't see anything.

Kill them. Asher frowned at how urgently his inner wolf had whispered that. Kill who? There was no one there. *Protect her.* Asher shook his head hard. His wolf was clearly in the first stages of madness. Maybe this was how it was for Gentry and Roman. Maybe the instinct to covet and protect got overwhelming around an interesting female.

Interesting female? That didn't feel right. Ashlyn was taking up every thought he had right now. A wolf howled in the distance, and for some reason, it made him angry. It felt directed at him, though it had to be miles away. He didn't recognize the voice, but then again, he hadn't been around the Bone-Rippers enough to have their songs memorized. Maybe the pack was hunting tonight. That's probably why his wolf was worked up.

Kill them.

Jesus. Asher linked his hands behind his head and tried to calm his instincts. They warred for him to stay posted right here, protecting Ashlyn's sleeping body from absolutely nothing, or going out into the woods and starting another war with all the damn wolves in Rangeley to get them to shut the fuck up. Ashlyn was tired. He didn't want them to wake her up.

Kill them before they hurt her. Asher's wolf was scratching at his skin now, making his flesh tingle with the first phase of the Change. He needed to calm down. There was nothing in the woods that would hurt her. He was the only danger here.

Ashlyn made a soft sleep sound that resembled a happy sigh. Asher forced his gaze away from the woods outside and turned, gazed at Ashlyn. The blue moonlight highlighted her pretty cheekbones, and right now, her long lashes were resting on her cheeks, and her lips were relaxed into an almost smile. Of course she probably smiled in her sleep. She was naturally happy. *Mine.* He tested the thought just to see if a creature of darkness like him had the ability to feel something real for a woman like her.

He needed to leave but couldn't make his legs move toward the door. Instead, just to see if he could without hurting her, Asher moved two deliberate steps closer to the bed. The blue around her was pulsing, calling to him. Two more steps, and he reached out and touched the bed. Two more steps, and his knees brushed the edge of the mattress. She let off the cutest fucking sleep sound he'd ever heard and rolled toward him.

Ashlyn slept right in the middle of the bed, and that told him two things. One, she was a bed hog. And two, she hadn't slept with a man in her bed for a while, so she was probably single. A soft, satisfied rumble worked its way up his throat, but he cut it off so he wouldn't wake her. God, what was that noise? His wolf had practically purred like a damn housecat.

He wasn't hungry. The Taker was sleeping still. Maybe he could just touch the blue.

Asher sat carefully on the edge of the bed, ready to bolt from the room if she stirred. She didn't. She smiled in her sleep and scooted closer by inches. He liked to think he drew her in, like she was doing to him.

Ghosts were lining the room now, staring at them, waiting for...something.

Asher dragged his gaze down her body. She wore a thin-strapped nightgown and had shoved the covers down to her hips. She slept on her side, a pillow encased between her knees. He'd never been jealous of a pillow before, but there it was. Carefully, he leaned forward and ran his palm against the edge of the blue. It pulsed again and wrapped around his hand, all the way up his forearm.

And still...The Taker slumbered.

He was breathing too fast, and his heart was banging against his chest like a war drum. He scooted closer and brushed a curl from her cheek as gently as he could. The corner of her full lips lifted in a quick smile. The blue had crawled up to his shoulder, but he wasn't feeding on it. It was hard to breathe.

She made him feel good. Quieted the wolf in him, quieted the black fog. Ashlyn took up all of his attention, every bit of his focus.

And still...The Taker slumbered.

Impossible. Impossible that he could be this close

to a woman for this long. This close to an aura that would taste of freedom and happiness, and still he didn't want to eat her up. He wanted to touch her skin instead.

Losing his mind completely, Asher laid down gently beside her, facing her. He rested his knee on her pillow—the one between her knees. The blue stretched around him like an embrace, covering him completely. The buzz of magic in his head died to nothing. The constant snarl of his wolf died to nothing.

And still...The Taker slumbered.

He would just lay here for a little while, and watch her face while she slept. He would just lay here and feel the blue without devouring it. It was like rain on thirsty soil, and his skin prickled with a pleasurable sensation where it touched him. He closed his eyes as the hollowness inside of him faded away. Just a few minutes, and he would leave her to sleep in peace, because he couldn't fall asleep beside her. The Taker would wake up and want her. He could drain her dry in her sleep without him even waking up, and something about that made him hate The Taker inside of him even more.

Ashlyn was giving him a few moments of peace. Okay, perhaps giving wasn't the right word. He was stealing a few moments of peace from her. Still, he owed her protection. From himself.

Just a few minutes, and he would leave her alone.

Swallowing hard, Asher eased closer and rested his hand on the curve of her waist. He could feel her hipbone through the thin material of her nightgown. God, she was beautiful. She looked like an angel here in the dark, blanketed by that pretty blue. Blanketing him in that same blue. Angels and demons weren't a match.

Asher's eyes grew heavy, and his body relaxed muscle by muscle as he watched her sleep.

Just a few minutes, and he would leave her alone.

Just a few minutes of quiet.

Just a few minutes more.

And still…The Taker slumbered.

FIVE

So warm. Ashlyn scrunched up her nose and stretched, then moved closer to the warmth that snuggled against her back.

That warmth had a boner.

Her eyes flew open, and she looked down at the giant muscular arm that was draped across her waist. Yep, those were Asher's tattoos on the hand. What the hell had happened last night? *Oh my gosh, did we...?*

No.

Asher was sexy, and she hadn't taken a single sip of alcohol last night, so she would've definitely remembered sex with him. Plus, he was twice her weight. Literally. Sex with him would've squished her like a caterpillar, and she was still breathing.

Well, now what?

Asher groaned softly and rested his morning wood more securely against her butt. And her body, that little ho, arched back against him like a happy cat being petted.

His hand went from relaxed to gripping her waist in an instant. When he pulled her against his hips, her stomach did huge flip-flops with how fucking sexy this was.

It helped that she couldn't see his face here in the gray light of dawn. He was behind her, and this felt safer. She was free to let him touch her because she could pretend this wasn't real.

When his lips pressed onto the back of her neck, though, she was done. A small whimper crawled up her throat, and she rolled her hips back again and pulled the covers over their waists. Without a second of hesitation, Asher slid his hand down her thigh, then up her nightgown and into the front of her panties.

As he pushed his finger into her, she softly moaned, "Asher."

He tensed, but then shoved his other arm under

her, wrapped it around her waist and pulled her back against him, hard. There was a soft sound in his throat as he sucked on the back of her neck. A wild sound. She liked it.

Out of desperation for him to go faster, she rested her hand over his between her legs, but he bit her gently, and the feral sound got a bit louder. *Let me.* She could almost hear his words whispering through her mind. Chills lifted on her skin, and if she hadn't been in the throes of passion, perhaps that instinct would've made her more careful with him. But as it stood, he was very, very good at what he was doing between her thighs, and she'd lost her damn mind completely.

She was close already, spurred on by his hard erection bucking against her back. God, he was so close to her, but so far away, separated by clothes. She hated their clothes. She wanted to burn them for keeping them apart.

"More," she whispered.

Asher shook his head against the back of her neck in denial, his beard rasping against her sensitive skin.

They were moving together now, him against her back, her hips rolling against his hand. So natural. So good. Ashlyn let off a helpless sound every time his finger went deep enough and his hand touched her clit. He added a second finger, and she reached up over her shoulder, gripped the back of his neck, and closed her eyes to the world. Closed her eyes to everything so she could savor this incredible erotic sensation this man was filling her with.

Asher was grinding so hard against her back now, faster, jerkier. He had to be close, too, and it got her off even more. He plunged his fingers into her again and again, and she was done. Gone. Floating. When the first deep pulses of her orgasm blasted through her body, she cried out.

Asher eased off her back just enough to move his pants down and ruck her nightgown up to her shoulders. When he pressed against her again, she could feel his dick. So hard, and his strokes were fast and powerful against her spine. And as her aftershocks intensified, warmth spilled from him and coated her back. God, this was so hot. The sound in his throat was sexy as hell, and she'd never had an orgasm this blindingly pleasurable.

"Fuck," he growled out as he froze against her back, his dick still throbbing. In a rush, he bolted from the bed. One second he was wrapped around her body, cradling her, hand in her panties, fingers inside of her, every inch of his torso pressed against her back. And then, he was just...gone.

Ashlyn turned around and frowned at the door, but Asher was already out of the room. He'd fled like his tail had been set on fire. Great bouncing gonads, that man was fast. If she hadn't been covered in Asher-juice right now, she would've tried to convince herself she'd just had an erotic dream or something.

She started to feel sick. Nauseous sick. The kind that made her curl into herself and retch. Right behind her eyes was a stabbing pain of a headache, and her muscles ached like she'd run three miles.

Dizzy, she lay there staring at the door. She didn't want to move for fear of everything going haywire again. Her skin was covered in a cold sweat, and she couldn't stop shaking if her life depended on it.

And then just like that, the hurt stopped. Just...vanished. Carefully, Ashlyn sat up, clutching the covers to her chest.

What the hell had just happened? She hadn't fooled around with a stranger like that since college. She'd deemed that time period the Scandalous Years.

But all Asher had to do was almost kiss her last night and then lie against her this morning, and she buckled?

That man was some kind of magic.

Frowning so deeply her face hurt, she stood with the covers still wrapped around her like a burrito, and she padded to the door. She closed it gently and stepped back. There was a black duffle bag in the corner she hadn't noticed last night. Crap. This wasn't the guest room after all. This must've been Asher's room.

Cheeks on fire, she bustled into the on suite bathroom and turned on the tap water. She kept waiting for that dirty feeling to show up—the one where she'd gone too far with a boy and had regrets—but it didn't appear. Strange, because Asher had bolted like he couldn't get away from her fast enough. She should feel mortified right now, but mostly, she was just baffled by the man.

Why had he been sleeping beside her? Bitey, growly, mysterious man, who made her body revolt just by leaving her—Asher was an enigma she was suddenly desperate to learn more about.

But she shouldn't. This wasn't about her chasing a

guy. This trip was about Blaire, and Ashlyn couldn't get snared into staying here longer out of curiosity for Asher.

She needed to shower, meet up with Blaire and her new-best-friend-Mila, eat some pancakes, and focus on dragging Blaire back to civilization.

Gentry was a magician, clearly, who mucked with Blaire's mind.

Roman was a mouthy nudist.

And Asher was the scariest of all. He was too interesting for his own good, too sexy, and too beguiling.

The sooner Ashlyn got Blaire on the road to the airport and escaped this weird-ass town, the better.

She showered and readied for the day in a daze, her mind circling round and round what had happened in bed. Her body was still revved up, wanting more, desiring something she couldn't understand with a man who was utterly dangerous to her heart. He'd shown his colors. Asher Striker was a runner. She'd barely spoken to him, but already he'd run three times. The first few minutes she'd met him, he'd tried to escape into the house, then he'd almost kissed her in the dark and gone straight out the back door, and then there was this morning. That was an epic flee. Spooge on her back and then sprint for the door?

She needed to stop thinking about him asap.

Once she made it downstairs, hitting every damn, creaky board on the way down, the living room and kitchen were empty. Thank goodness! With a sigh of relief, she pulled on her pink jacket, flipped off the pink ski pants Asher had made fun of, then made her way out the front door as she wrapped a purple scarf around her neck.

She felt better the second she stepped out into the crisp mountain air. Inhaling noisily, she closed her eyes and let the wind touch her cheeks. This was good. Positive thinking conjured positive results. She could do this. Blaire would be convinced today how very un-normal her behavior was, and they would laugh about this over cocktails at their favorite bar back home in a month's time.

Shifting her oversize purse onto her shoulder, Ashlyn turned for the porch steps, but froze in her tracks when she spied the giant sitting on the swing. Asher was still, watching her with eyes such a light blue it was hard to look at them, and just as hard to look away.

He wore a black sweater that clung to the curves of his muscular arms. The neck was wider, showing a peek at a curve of ink she couldn't read under his left collarbone. His lips were pursed into a thin line under his blond beard, and his fair brows were lowered and troubled looking.

"H-hi," she said lamely.

"Are you okay?" His voice came out gruff, as if he hadn't used it in a while.

It was a strange question, and one she hadn't expected, so she shrugged up one shoulder. "What do you mean?"

"Are you sick?"

"Like perverted? I mean…maybe a little." Lie, she was one hundred percent perverted.

Asher's lip twisted up into a fast smile right before he ducked his gaze to the steaming mug of coffee cupped in his massive hands. He was hiding it, but she'd seen the hint of a grin, and something inside of her grew desperate to see it again.

"I meant, do you feel well this morning?" Nope, he wasn't even trying to look at her anymore.

She should go. Just…walk to her car and speed

out of the icy parking lot and not look back. But as rough around the edges as Asher seemed with his muscles and tattoos and his tendency to bolt the second things got real, he had been gentle during the almost kiss last night, and had made sure she had an orgasm before he took care of himself this morning. And he was sitting here, perhaps waiting for her, and asking if she was okay. To her, that counted for something. So Ashlyn went against her better judgement and made her way to the swing, hesitated only a moment before she sat beside him stiffly.

"I feel...confused."

Asher handed her the mug of coffee without looking at her. A peace offering? Or an apology perhaps because he wasn't responding.

Okay. She took the mug and tried again. "Was I sleeping in your bedroom?"

"My dad's bedroom," he said, twitching his head and staring out across the property toward a frozen lake.

"Where is your dad?"

Asher slid her an icy look, then flicked his gaze to something beside her before he gave his attention again to his clasped hands dangling between his knees.

For some reason, Ashlyn didn't want to turn around and look beside her. The temperature seemed to drop ten degrees in an instant, and instinctively, she scooted closer to Asher.

"What happened this morning..." He clenched his jaw and leveled her with that frosty blue look. "It was a mistake. A moment of weakness. You're so... I messed up, but I'll be more careful."

"Careful not to accidentally finger-bang me?" she teased nervously.

Asher jerked his chin to her coffee. "Drink. You're shivering."

"I don't like black coffee, remember?"

"Pretend it's hot chocolate."

"You're bossy."

"You probably haven't minded anyone in your whole life."

"I'm grown. Why would I need to mind anyone?" God, he was frustrating.

"If I gave you a warning...one that could save your life...would you mind me then?"

Well, that was different. "Maybe."

Asher looked sick when he said, "Stay away from

me."

And then he stood and made his way inside, leaving her swaying on the swing in a baffled daze.

And there it was. Again.

Asher Striker had just run for the fourth time.

SIX

"You've hardly touched any of your waffles," Blaire pointed out.

Ashlyn dragged her attention from the snowy scenery outside and made a show of cutting off another piece.

"Are you okay?" Blaire asked.

The answer was hell no. She was confused out of her mind by Asher. And she'd just listened to a fifteen-minute laugh-fest between Blaire and Mila about a dozen inside jokes that Ashlyn could only guess at, and she felt like the odd woman out. Again. She couldn't say that without turning the conversation weird, though, so instead she said, "It's really beautiful out here."

Mila cleared her throat delicately. "You should see it in the spring and summer. It's stunning. So green you wouldn't believe, and in the fall, we have some of the prettiest color changes in the leaves in the whole world. Tourists flock here just to see it."

Ashlyn smiled politely at her replacement. "That sounds nice."

Mila dipped her soft brown eyes to her plate. "I think I'm going to go to the bathroom. Give you two some time together." She gave an empty smile and excused herself.

"Do you not like Mila?" Blaire asked quietly. "She's trying."

"I'm sure she's fine, but you have to understand it from my perspective, Blaire. You just up and left me. Left. Me. You don't call or answer my texts half the time."

"Because there are things about my life you won't understand now, and I don't know how to talk to you."

"Great. Shut me out then, Blaire. That makes this so much easier. And then I come here, and you've got a new best friend and this new life, and you're so different."

"Different how?"

Ashlyn wanted to pop off. She wanted to call her naïve, but that word wouldn't feel right. Not since she'd noticed something else over breakfast, something that scared her even more. Something that made her think she really had lost her best friend. With a sigh, Ashlyn crossed her arms over her chest and murmured, "You seem happier. More self-assured. Less stressed. You even look refreshed. You smile a lot more, speak clearer, and I can tell the divorce is in your rearview mirror. I pushed for that for so long, but it took you coming here and meeting new friends to get to a good place. I guess I feel left behind."

Blaire's heart was in her eyes, and her bottom lip trembled like she was going to cry. Aw, crap. Ashlyn draped her arm around her shoulders and pulled her in close. She rested her cheek on top of Blaire's fiery hair and muttered, "This is the part where I'm supposed to bow out graciously, right? Where I'm supposed to be one hundred percent happy for you and pout quietly where you can't see it, because you deserve this happiness, Blaire. You deserve to find a man who treats you like a queen, and it seems like

Gentry does. I mean, it's kind of gross how he called up here and paid for the breakfast, but it's also pretty sweet, and they should put that shit in romantic movies. Springing for these terrible mimosas was a pretty slick move, too," she said, gesturing to the mason jar of orange juice and cheap champagne, the best Jack's had to offer. "I mean, Matt used to block us from having girl days, and Gentry seems to support you living your life, and—"

Blaire hugged her tight and nearly cut off her air. "He's amazing, Ashlyn. You'll see. Just stay a few days and really get to know the people here. You won't worry for me anymore, and we can just go back to the way things were. I'll do better about answering my phone, and everything will be okay. You'll see. I'm sorry."

And now Ashlyn was blinking back tears because Blaire's apology meant the world. She was the best friend she'd ever had.

"Look, the grand opening for Winter's Edge is happening in a week. Stay for that. Stay for the party! You can go back home after that, but maybe a week will give you enough time to get to know Gentry, Mila, and Roman."

Ashlyn narrowed her eyes. "And Asher."

"Eeeeee," Blaire said, easing away from her. "Asher's a good one to steer clear of."

"Uuuh, why? Because I know you're not just going to give me that little riddle and think I would leave it alone."

"He's just..." Blaire pursed her lips and rolled her eyes to the ceiling like she was searching for the right word. "Better when he's alone."

"Well, we fooled around this morning, so does that count as steering clear?"

"What?" Blaire barked out way too loud.

Ashlyn snorted. She'd always loved shocking Blaire. She got scandalized way too easily. "Not my fault."

"How is you fooling around with a rando not your fault," Blaire whisper screamed.

"He's not a rando, B. He's the hot brother of your someday baby daddy. We could be sisters."

"Oh my gosh." Blaire looked panicked as Mila sat down across the table from them.

"Everything okay?" Mila asked, concern pooling in her eyes.

"No," Blaire squeaked. "Ashlyn fooled around

with Asher—"

"Blaire!" Ashlyn admonished her. "For fuck's sake, I didn't want to tell the world."

"Wait, you and Asher?" Mila asked low, leaning forward. "Like…he willingly touched you?"

"Well, I don't have leprosy," Ashlyn scoffed.

"No, I'm not saying…shit, let me start over," Mila muttered. "Asher doesn't touch people."

"Well, I'm not people. I'm a voluptuous woman with a superior set of diddle-skills."

"No," Blaire said. "Ashlyn, we're serious. Asher doesn't do touch. I didn't even think he could. He's a little…"

"Terrifying," Mila said, finishing Blaire's sentence. Annoying.

"Well, he touched me just fine, and I had a monster fucking orgasm. He isn't terrifying, he's just mysterious, or misunderstood, or I don't know. You are both making me feel gross, and I shouldn't. I'm a grown woman who slept beside a man—"

"Wait, he slept by you?" Blaire hissed.

"Oh my God, move, I need out. I can't handle your judgement right now. You! The one who moved in with a man after you knew him for, like, fifteen seconds."

"That's not what I mean. I'm not judging!"

Blaire was blocking her from getting out, but Ashlyn was good and pissed, so okay, she would just go under the table. Stupid big tits got in the way as she slid down between the booth and the edge of the table. Squishing her boobs down, she melted off the booth and onto the floor, where she bumped her head and crawled across the tile, shoving Blaire and Mila's legs out of the way as she went.

Blaire grabbed her arm as she scrambled for the door, and damn, she was a lot stronger than Ashlyn remembered.

"Ash, I'm not judging. I'm saying to be careful, but if Asher can touch you, it's a big deal."

"Not polite."

"No, I mean it's a big deal for him. Really, really big." Blaire arched her ruddy brows and gave her a serious look.

Ashlyn stood and dusted off her knees, cleared her throat, and straightened her scarf. "I want to know what's going on."

Blaire parted her lips to say something, but Mila murmured, "Blaire. Don't."

And her friend's response was instant. Regret pooled in the green depths of her eyes, and she shook her head and shrugged an apology. "I wish I could tell you everything."

"Yeah." Ashlyn swallowed hard. "Me, too." Because being on the outside really sucked.

"Will you please stay until the grand opening of Winter's Edge?" Blaire asked. "Please. I like having you here. I've missed you, and I really want you to see my life here so you don't worry."

Ashlyn smiled sadly and nodded. "Sure."

Blaire squeezed her hand, and then she and Mila led the way outside, Ashlyn trailing behind, feeling like the dirt under the concrete, under the ice, under the layer of snow in Jack's parking lot.

She waved to the girls, who piled in an old truck, and then made her way to her rental car, but stopped when she noticed the tires. Her smart car now sported chains on the tires, and one giant man dressed in a skin-tight black sweater was fastening the back one.

"Asher?"

He looked up with a wholly unsurprised look, then stood and dusted snow from his hands.

Gesturing to the chains, he said in a gravelly voice, "Now you're less likely to die."

"Huh. Romantic."

"I wasn't trying for that. It was just…well, I needed you to be safer."

"This is better than a boy buying me flowers."

Asher frowned deeply. "Stop that."

But she was having too much fun with his discomfort. "First you jizz on my back—"

"I said stop. I don't want to do this." With long, graceful strides, he made his way to a black Tundra pickup truck with black rims.

Ashlyn power-walked to keep up. "How did you get the chains on? I thought you had to back a car over them."

"I lifted your car over them."

She glared at the back of his head and waited for the punchline, but none came. "You lifted up my car?"

Asher tossed her an icy look over his shoulder and opened his door. "It weighs about three pounds, so it wasn't that hard."

Frustrating man, running again, but she wasn't having it. She bolted for the driver's side and scrambled into the seat before Asher could. When he stood staring at her with shock in his frosty eyes, she grinned ridiculously big and buckled up. "Get in, Striker. I'm driving."

"Get out."

"No! You get in."

The soft, wild sound he made filled the air, but he cut it off fast.

"Growl all you want to. That just reminds me of your finger-fuck-and-run, and makes me horny."

Asher ran his hand through his hair and looked furious as he glared at Jack's. "You aren't supposed to say no!"

"No," she said primly, gripping the steering wheel. She arched her eyebrow at him. "Get. In."

Asher slammed the door, and then muttered to himself as he stomped around the front of the truck. And then he yanked open the passenger side door, folded himself inside, buckled up, and rested his elbow on the window, biting his thumbnail.

"Where to?" she asked, highly amused by his mantrum.

"You wanted to drive!"

"Whoo, you're letting me plan our first date."

"It's not a date."

"Keys, boyfriend."

Asher shook his head for a long time before he reached into his back pocket and slapped a pair of keys onto her palm. They were black with no keychain at all. Why was she not surprised?

"Want to see my keychain?"

"No."

She pulled hers out. There were approximately two dozen brightly-colored keychains, bottle openers, and miniature stuffed animals on hers.

Asher looked disgusted. "How do you even find your keys on that thing."

"I like searching. I get to see all this stuff that makes me happy every time I turn my car on or let myself into my apartment."

"I didn't mean to *jizz* on your back. I just meant to take care of you, but you smell good, and your hair is pretty, and you felt good against my dick."

She smiled brightly. "Did you just call me beautiful?"

Asher turned up the radio, so she pitched her voice louder as she continued. "Because I think you're beautiful, too! In that slightly psychotic, terrifying, he-might-or-might-not-be-a-serial-killer type of way.

You have nice eyes. Well, actually, you have super-mean eyes, but they are a nice color. Do you like creamy peanut butter or crunchy?"

"What?" he asked, his voice tainted with irritation.

Ashlyn turned the steering wheel with one hand and turned down the rock music with the other. "Creamy or crunchy, and don't be flippant about your answer, Striker. This could be a deal breaker for me."

"Mother fucker." Asher heaved a sigh. "Creamy."

"Thank goodness." Ashlyn wiped pretend sweat from her brow and grinned at him. "I thought we were done before we started there for a second."

His lip almost, almost twitched into a smile. Good, she was on the right track with him.

"Ideal date?"

"Pass, Sparkles."

"Whoa, a nickname? You must really like me. Fine, I will tell you mine. I want some hot cabana boy to feed me grapes and seduce me and spend all day in bed with me making me feel like a goddess. Age?"

Asher cracked his knuckles. "I don't like talking about personal stuff."

"Oh my gosh, stop being weird. How old are you?"

"Twenty-seven."

She made a disappointed click sound behind her teeth. "I'm thirty. Probably way too old and mature for you. You're making me feel like a cougar right now."

Asher cleared his throat and carefully said, "Because you find me attractive?"

"Hot-as-fuck attractive. Yes. I mean, you probably work out like eight hours a day and are most likely super-conceited about your body, but you have tattoos and a beard and pretty eyes, and I dig blonds, apparently, so take my panties already, Striker."

Asher snorted and looked out his window, hiding his face. She could see the curve of his cheek, though. He was smiling. "Perverted old lady."

She scoffed and turned left onto the main drag in Rangeley. "I'm never letting you dry hump my back again."

"Stop," he said, but his voice wasn't mad anymore. It was amused.

He'd arranged his face into a bored mask by the time he turned toward her again. He gestured to her one-handed turning of the wheel. "Where did you learn to drive a big truck?"

"I learned on an old Dodge Ram my grandpa gave me for my sixteenth birthday. He told me if I could learn to drive that old thing, I would be able to drive anything. It had ten tricks just to get it started."

"What color?"

"Cream and red and rust. Lots of rust," she said, casting him a quick grin. "There was a hole in the floorboard I would get my heel stuck in sometimes. My grandpa taught me how to drive it." Ashlyn frowned as she considered telling him the deep, not-so-happy part of the story.

"Say it," Asher said, as if he could read her hesitation.

Ashlyn inhaled deeply and parked the truck right in front of a coffee shop with a wood-burning stove out on the sprawling side-porch. "My grandpa passed away a year after he gave me the truck. I drove that thing into the ground until I couldn't fix it any more. It was my favorite car ever because…"

"Because it was his."

"Yeah."

Asher pulled something out from under the neck of his shirt. It was a thin strip of leather, and on the end of the necklace was a carved wooden wolf.

Ashlyn turned off the truck and asked, "Can I touch it?"

After only a moment of hesitation, Asher dipped his chin once.

She held the wolf gently and rubbed her finger over the polished wood. "Was it your dad's?"

Another dip of his chin.

She had to know, because this felt big. "Have you ever shown this to anyone?"

"No," Asher said in that sexy, deep timbre of his. "Things were complicated with my father. My feelings about him...well, they're complicated, too."

Ashlyn, tucked the necklace gently back into the neck of his shirt and rested her hand over the pendant there. "I won't tell anyone."

"Truth," he said, his eyebrows lifting slightly in surprise. "You're good at secrets then?"

"Secrets are kind of my forte." She tossed him a saucy look, then pushed the door open and slid out of the jacked-up truck.

"What do you mean by that?" he asked, getting out of the truck as she made her way around the front.

"My dad liked to drink. He was loud and

embarrassing on whiskey, and I learned real quick that keeping secrets and distancing myself from people at school made everything easier." She slipped on the second stair, but Asher's hand was instantly on her back, propping her up. She smiled her thanks and gripped the inside of his elbow without invitation.

Asher's eyes went round, and he dipped his shocked gaze to where her pink mitten contrasted with his black sweater. There was a moment where he looked panicked—as though he would bolt right back to the truck and leave her here. But he didn't pluck her off him. Instead, he helped her stay steady up the slippery steps and opened the door for her like a gentleman. Hmmm, she liked this man. Rough, quiet, and a little scary, but with manners.

Inside, it was warm, thanks to a fireplace on the far wall. The flames heated the small coffee shop. It looked like an old country store with rough wooden walls and a plethora of cartoon pig-themed gifts and cookware. The line was six deep, and Asher looked uncomfortable as hell standing in the crowded room. He sidled away from anyone who stepped too close, and once he made that strange sound in his throat when a man bumped her shoulder on accident as he exited the shop.

Clearly, Asher wasn't a social butterfly, so to ease his tension, she leaned close and talked low. "I was an only child, and I had to keep my dad's shortcomings secret so I could keep my family together. My parents were all I had, so I put up with a lot to protect that. Now you go."

"Go where?" he asked, his gaze on her hand gripping his arm again.

"I mean your turn, you share something."

"I already told you I like creamy peanut butter and my age. You're pushing."

"Holy hell balls, Asher, tell me something silly then. Tell me your favorite color."

"Black."

She gave him a dead-eyed look.

"Second favorite is dark gray, but so dark it's almost black."

The man was exhausting. "Favorite hobby?"

"Surveillance."

She blinked slowly. "What does that even mean? Like stalking?"

"No." He smiled for just an instant, and it was breathtaking. Just a flash of white teeth, and then his face settled into a passive expression again. "I work in surveillance. Cameras, audio, some investigative work."

"Like a private investigator?"

His eyes narrowed to icy blue slits. "Kind of. No cheating spouses or thieving nannies, though. My clients are a little more...dangerous."

"Oh," she murmured. "Sounds terrifying. Well I work a super-dangerous job, too, Striker."

"Oh, yeah? What do you do?" At least he looked more relaxed now, and they were almost to the front of the line.

"I work as a junior acquisitions editor for a paretty big publisher."

"Sounds treacherous."

"Oh, it is. Papercuts galore, and there's this guy a couple floors below me who basically stalks me. He tried to kiss me in an elevator once."

Asher's lip lifted in a quick snarl before he smoothed his expression back into place again. That one look sent chills up her spine, though. It had transformed his face into something almost animal. "He tries to kiss you without you inviting him to?"

"Yep. Don't worry about me, Young Buck. I keep a

pocket knife in my purse."

"Let me see it."

She pulled out the tiny black knife she'd practiced flicking open for half an hour in the store before she got the hang of it. "Told you I was dangerous."

"Mmmm," Asher said, reaching into his back pocket. He pulled out a big knife, the handle black with white skulls. "Trade me."

Holy shit! She was trying to be cool and have a poker face, but that was one big-ass blade. "Trade you for that? The skulls aren't my style."

Asher flicked the black blade open. It looked really sharp, and part of the blade was serrated. "Ignore the skulls. That little toothpick won't keep you safe from anything or anyone. This one will. What is that asshole's last name?" Asher asked, pushing the blade back into the handle.

"Um, no, PI. I'm not giving you his name. You just told me you stalk people for a living, and you pulled out a freaking machete. Being a murderer is kind of a deal breaker for me."

"Fine. I won't hunt him if you trade me knives."

Irritating. "Fine," she ground out. "It will probably take me three days to even learn how to open this without chopping my fingers—"

Asher gripped her hand, pushed her finger on a lever, and flicked her wrist. Out swung the blade, smooth-as-you-like. He showed her how to lock it back into the handle and then pocketed the small black one she'd given him in exchange. When Ashlyn looked up, the couple in front of them was staring like she and Asher had just turned to necromancers and raised a corpse.

"What?" Asher growled. Good with people, he was not.

"Are you fucking kidding?" the woman asked, her eyes flashing with anger. "You know the rules." Her blue eyes slid to Ashlyn, then back to Asher. "You know what she is."

The man she was with warned her, "Amanda."

"Uh, what am I?" Ashlyn asked the rude skank.

"You're not good enough," she answered without a single second of hesitation. She leveled Asher with a disgusted look. "You fuckin' Strikers. You just can't stay away from them, can you?" She shook her head and huffed a breath. "You have no idea what's coming for you."

The woman bent suddenly, clutching her

stomach, and the lights above them flickered. And then Ashlyn was feeling sick, too, nauseous like this morning. When the lights dimmed dangerously, like the bulbs would pop, the people around them started talking in panicked voices. Asher stared at Amanda with a dead expression in his eyes and a wicked smirk on his lips.

Ashlyn was going to retch, but she couldn't seem to move to run to the bathroom. "Asher?" she asked helplessly.

Asher jerked his attention to her, and the lights came back full illumination. And just like that, the wave of sickness was gone.

"Let's go," the man said to Amanda, gripping her elbow and guiding her past them.

"I know what you are," Amanda whispered furiously as they passed. She made the sign of the devil as fury roiled in her eyes.

Asher looked completely unoffended by that. In fact, he had no reaction other than to step forward, take their place in line, and order a black coffee for himself. And then he gestured Ashlyn to the counter and said, "What do you want, Sparkles? I'm sure it'll be pink in color and taste like cotton candy." There was an edge to his voice she didn't understand. It was hard, and sharp as a razor.

Baffled by what had just happened, she clasped her shaking hands in front of her and ordered her peppermint, white chocolate mocha.

Asher didn't say a word as they waited for their order, and he remained silent as they made their way outside and sat in a pair of rocking chairs by the warm wood-burning fireplace.

"Why were you upset about me ordering a pink drink?"

"Order what you like, it doesn't matter to me."

"Lie."

"You can't tell if someone's lying."

"But you can?"

Asher took a sip of his coffee and gave her a warning look. His eyes looked even lighter blue now.

"Aren't you cold?" she asked, gesturing to his thin sweater. He wasn't even wearing gloves.

"No."

"When the lights flickered inside—"

"No."

"When Amanda said I wasn't good enough—"

"No."

Asher reminded her of Blaire with all the secrets. "This is exactly what I don't need."

"Agreed."

"You don't even know what I'm talking about! I'm losing my best friend, Asher. My best friend. She's like my sister. I was lonely, and then Blaire came along, and I haven't been lonely a day in my life since. Until she came here and didn't come back home. Didn't come back to me. And now she's full of secrets. I was so upset when I was leaving Jack's, feeling utterly rejected, and there you were. This beautiful distraction. And what have you done? You've made me feel the exact same way as Blaire did. I hate this place."

"I hate it, too."

"Then why are you here?"

"Because my dad died, and I had to come back to spread his ashes."

The candid way he dropped that information bomb drew her up short. "Your dad died? When?"

"A couple of months ago."

"Have you spread his ashes?"

Asher huffed a humorless laugh. "Kind of."

"Yet, you're still here. In this place you claim to

hate."

"It's not a claim, it's a fact. I don't belong here. Never did."

"So what are you still doing in Rangeley?"

"Waiting, and seeing."

God, he was impossible. "Waiting for what?" she gritted through her teeth.

He leveled her with a cool look. "Waiting to see if this town will go up in flames. Waiting to see if my brothers will need me. Waiting to see if Blaire or Mila will need me. My job isn't finished here."

She was so confused. "Your surveillance job?"

"No."

Ashlyn sighed in frustration. She was being talked in circles and couldn't seem to stop the ride. "Do *you* think I'm not good enough for you?"

"You're plenty good enough for me, Ashlyn." He canted his head, dragged his gaze down her body, then back up, and locked onto her eyes. "But you're making me feel different, and it's dangerous."

"Dangerous how?"

Asher let of a soft growl. "I have seasoned and haunted my soul to perfection. I don't need fixing. I need you to stop touching my artwork."

Ashlyn felt slapped by his words. On one hand, they were kind of beautiful, but she hadn't been trying to fix anyone. She couldn't even fix herself. "I don't understand what you mean."

"Forget it. I just meant it's me who's not good for you."

Okay, this had gone too serious, way too fast. "But we both like creamy peanut butter." She slipped a tiny smile onto her lips to show she was teasing.

Asher leaned forward and rested his elbows on his knees, studied her with a calculating look. "I was angry at your drink choice because you're so different from me."

Ashlyn tucked her knees up to her chest and faced him in the chair. "You don't like us being different?"

"Not this different. I don't change. I don't get better, or lighter, or easier. Amanda mentioned the rules. I'm not supposed to be with you. Not even as friends. And I would fight the rules and say fuck it except for you're peppermint, white chocolate mocha, and I'm coffee black. And even if you amuse me, and even if I think about you when you're not around, and even if I want to know more about you, protect you, and touch you, I can see clearly where we're headed."

"And where's that?"

Asher swallowed hard. Such honesty pooled in the bright blue of his eyes as he whispered, "Nowhere."

SEVEN

Asher had sufficiently confused Ashlyn into a stupor. She couldn't think straight as she put her clothes away in the chest of drawers in Asher's room. Yep, she was claiming this room for sentimental reasons. Their early morning fool-around session seemed so long ago now, but it had meant something to her. She hadn't been touched like that by a man in a while. Not just physically, but he'd done something strange to her heart. To her mind. He'd attached her to him somehow.

Something was strangely in Rangeley though. Something big. With every minute she stayed, and every encounter she had with the Strikers, with Mila, the people of this town, and even Blaire, her instincts kicked up at the wrongness a little more. And at the top of that mountain of mystery sat one badass, tatted-up, behemoth of a man named Asher.

Why did she always do this? Bad boys were her Achilles heel. She'd always gone for the ones destined to break her heart. Blaire had always said it was because Ashlyn didn't want to settle down—not really. The bad boys would break her heart, and she would move on because that was how she thought love was supposed to be—an endless loop of breathtaking excitement and butterflies and then bone-deep, soul-deep, heart-deep pain when they left for something better, somewhere better...someone better.

Asher had been right. They would go nowhere. She'd been on this roller coaster loop before, and while it was exciting for a moment, it always ended too soon.

A week was what she'd promised Blaire. She had plenty of time off work saved up, so okay, she would stay and make sure Blaire was all right in her new life, and she would go to the bar opening. But she would avoid the hell out of one sexy, icy-eyed mystery man who had apparently taken lessons on how to make a woman fall into serious lust with one above-average finger-bang.

That was all this was—lust.

A soft knock sounded at the door, and she twisted around to see Mila standing timidly in the hallway. "Hey."

Ashlyn closed the drawer and forced a smile. "Hey."

"Soooo, I wanted to talk to you. Is it okay if I come in?"

"Sure."

Mila entered, dark hair twitching with her graceful gait, and she sat on the edge of the unmade bed. "This morning was awkward."

"Awkward as fuck," Ashlyn agreed, resting her back against the dresser.

"And I've been thinking about it a lot. Too much, maybe, about how I would feel in your shoes, and I kind of hate that I'm probably a big part of the problem. I'm not trying to replace you as Blaire's best friend, Ashlyn. She talks about you all the time. I feel like I already know you just from her stories. So I thought if you maybe knew a little about me, I would be less of a threat?"

"Crunchy or creamy peanut butter?" Ashlyn asked, narrowing her eyes.

"Crunchy," Mila said without a second thought.

Ashlyn hissed and shook her head. "I don't know if we can bury the hatchet now, Mila. That's a deal-breaker."

Mila giggled. "I would switch my favorite if we could make this easier on Blaire."

Hmm. Ashlyn liked that. She began to make the bed, and Mila stood up and helped on the other side.

"I have been stuck in this town for a long time, and I didn't really have girlfriends. Not good ones. I was really lonely until Blaire came along. She's amazing."

"That she is," Ashlyn agreed, straightening the sheet.

"I was thinking maybe we should do some fun stuff together. I mean, I'm totally cool with letting you have Blaire all to yourself as much as you want, but if you…you know…want to hang out with me, too, I would like that. I think you're funny, and I keep laughing at the memory of you crawling under the table at Jack's. Everyone was staring, but you didn't care at all, and I liked it. I want to be more like that."

Mila was blushing hard, her cheeks the color of cherries, and she wouldn't meet Ashlyn's eyes. Mila was a shy girl. Blaire had gone shy when her ex-husband had wrecked her with that divorce, and something about Mila's discomfort pulled at Ashlyn's protective instincts. Dammit.

"Anyway," Mila rushed out. "I have ideas if you want to do fun stuff. I'm gonna let you get back to unpacking."

She rushed toward the door, but Ashlyn called, "Waaaait."

Mila turned, wringing her hands in front of her lap. "Yeah?"

Ashlyn sighed in irritation that she was really going to reach out and take this olive branch. She'd wanted to hang onto her jealousy for a while longer. Grudges weren't fun if they ended too quickly. "What did you have in mind?"

Mila's soft chocolate-colored eyes flickered up to hers, then down to the ground again as a smile stretched her lips. "I was going to teach Blaire bartending tricks today. I know a lot of of them, like spinning bottles, and doing lines of shots all at once. I can even blow fire. Soooo…I was wondering if you wanted to learn with her? We can do it when the boys are out so they won't be pissed if we break bottles behind the bar."

"That actually sounds kind of awesome because I'm in desperate need of new party tricks. Tying cherry stems with my tongue isn't getting me laid anymore."

Mila's eyes went round, and she huffed a surprised-sounding laugh. "I can teach you stuff to get you laid," she teased so quietly it was almost a whisper.

"My vagina thanks you," Ashlyn murmured.

Mila laughed and pressed her hands on her cheeks as if trying to cool them. "When do you want to do it?"

"I'm free now. Plus, I know Blaire is trying to work on some manuscripts, and I like to corrupt her and make her a terrible employee, so let's go bully her into playing."

"Okay," Mila said with a shy smile.

Blaire wasn't even that hard to convince away from her work, which told Ashlyn something important. She was happier here, living life more. Back home, she'd been obsessed with work just to escape the unhappiness of her divorce. But New Blaire wasn't necessarily bad. She was different, sure, but maybe she'd needed that.

As a trio, they stepped out onto the porch of Blaire's cabin she shared with Gentry, and then they made their way down the stairs to the icy parking lot. Blaire led them to a worn trail in the woods and explained, "This is the back way to Winter's Edge."

"And that's the bar Asher's dad ran before he passed away?"

Blaire shot her a strange look.

"What?" Ashlyn asked.

"Nothing."

"Spill, Red," she demanded, using the nickname she called Blaire when she was being ridiculous.

"I just find it interesting that you said Asher's dad, instead of Gentry or Roman's dad."

"It's not interesting. He's the one I've talked to the most."

"Yeah, talked to," Blaire said, poking a finger through a hole she made with her other hand.

"That's enough, you perv. It was a beautiful experience, and you're just jealous."

"Of fooling around with Asher? You're lucky

you're still alive." There was a hard edge to Blaire's voice.

"He's not that scary, just so you know."

Blaire called her out. "You say that about every terrifying person you date."

"Maybe I'm just tougher than the average broad and can manage the monsters better."

"Not this monster," Mila murmured so quietly Ashlyn almost missed it.

She parted her lips to make fun of them both for being pussies, but both Mila and Blaire jerked their gazes to the exact same spot in the woods at once. They stood there frozen like garden statues in the middle of the winter forest.

Chills lifted on Ashlyn's body. She strained her ears and searched the woods, but heard and saw nothing out of the ordinary. What the hell was going on?

When Blaire ripped her gaze from the woods and looked behind them, her eyes looked strange in the evening light. Ashlyn turned to follow her attention. Asher strode toward them, his eyes on the woods where Mila was still staring.

A howl rose on the wind, long and loud. Ashlyn's

heartrate jacked up ten notches. "What the hell? There's a wolf out here?" Or please God, let Blaire reassure her that was a coyote.

"Go on," Asher rumbled in a gravelly voice. "It's fine. He's probably just curious."

Unable to get her legs moving, Ashlyn asked him, "What's happening?" as Asher approached.

Mila and Blaire were already moving through the woods, following the trail slowly as Asher caught up. He gripped her arm and got her moving easily enough—by practically dragging her.

Ashlyn shoved off him and frowned. Asher didn't seem to mind her balking, though. He just walked beside her, placing himself between her and the forest where the howl had sounded.

Now she felt guilty for taking his good knife, which was sitting in her purse inside of the cabin. All he had to defend them was her little black knife, which was really no weapon at all.

He lifted his nose in the air and sniffed, then bent smoothly, picked up a handful of snow, and released it into the wind. It blew east, and he murmured mysteriously, "Clever."

"What's clever?"

"Staying downwind."

Whatever that meant. Through the trees loomed a big log cabin with a sign over the door that read Winter's Edge. Blaire led them right through the clearing and to a side door, and then she and Mila disappeared inside.

Asher gripped Ashlyn's elbow before she followed, easing her to a stop. "Nothing will hurt you. I'll make sure of it." His voice had gone deadly serious. She believed him because, clearly, he believed every word he told her. His Adam's apple dipped low into his muscular neck as he swallowed, and with a passive look in his blazing eyes, he murmured, "I'm sorry about earlier."

"Oh, you mean about telling me we were headed nowhere, as if I'd asked you to define our relationship, and then ignoring me the entire way back to my car? Forgiven, I guess, Stranger. But even if I was in the mood to put up with your man-shenanigans—"

Asher leaned down and kissed her into silence. It was a hard kiss, a painful one. One where his teeth grazed her lips before he pushed his tongue past without invitation and stroked unapologetically against her tongue. He gripped the back of her neck too hard. Rough man. She bit his bottom lip to punish his carelessness.

A sexy sound snarled from him, and he shoved her back against the wall of Winter's Edge. He'd stunned her again, and her traitor body was so revved up now, she stopped fighting him, stopped her biting him again. Asher gripped the back of her hair and angled her face up, disengaged their kiss, and dragged his lips to her neck where he sucked hard. He ground his body against hers, nearly suffocating her. She was half his size, and apparently he wasn't in the mood for gentleness like this morning.

"I can't fucking stop thinking about you," he rasped against her neck. "I'm going crazy. I know I am. You're making me crazy. Fffuck." He pushed off her and splayed his hands on either side of her face, trapping her against the wall. His eyes were so pretty right now, such a light blue. His chest was heaving as he dragged in breath after frozen breath, eyes locked on hers, gaze intense. She would've given her bones to hear what he was thinking right now, but when she asked, he shook his head and answered, "Nothing good. You call to me. It's a dangerous game for both of us."

Riddles, riddles, riddles. Did the man know that telling her she should stay away from him only make her stubborn streak wider? She liked disobedience. So she slid her hands up his strong chest and wrapped her arms around his neck, leaned up on her tiptoes, and pressed a kiss to the base of his throat. She could be seductive, too, and he deserved it. He'd been wrecking her hormones since she met him. A soft groan rattled his throat, vibrating against her moving lips. She smiled and sucked, then moved up to his jaw and gave it the same affection. Up, up until she reached his lips, and then she kissed him. Gently this time, and she didn't let him bully her into another hard kiss. She eased back every time he tried and shook her head until he was good and trained and eased forward, cupping the back of her head.

She ran her hands down his chest, down the defined mounds of his abs to the hem of his shirt. Lifting slightly, she brushed her fingers on his warm skin along his beltline. He shuddered like he was cold, but he couldn't be. His flesh was on fire, as if he had a fever.

Ashlyn eased her tongue past his lips and licked

him shallowly, and couldn't help the smile when he groaned a sexy, helpless sound. It was enough for now. Easing back, she disengaged with a soft smack and took her hands out from under his shirt.

"When you tell me to stay away from you, it only dares me to bring you in closer," she whispered. Ashlyn held his stunned gaze for a moment more, then ducked under his locked arm and went into Winter's Edge without a single look back.

Asher, Asher, the panty basher.

That man was all hard edges and sex-appeal, and it was becoming apparent he thought about her like she did him. He liked her body. She called to him without even trying.

She touched her throbbing lips with her fingertips as she followed the sound of the girl's voices into a big tavern room.

The howl lifted on the wind again, but for some reason, she wasn't scared this time. She didn't know why, but Asher's presence nearby made her feel safe in a way that made no sense.

That man had a darkness inside of him she would likely never understand. He kept it too closely guarded. She'd never met anyone like him, who had pulled at her heart so strongly, who had become interesting so quickly. But she knew by some instinct he was perfectly capable of handling whatever curious animal was outside if it decided to come too close.

Ashlyn was glad of his protective instincts because she was certain she'd hate being on Asher's bad side.

EIGHT

Something was wrong.

Asher narrowed his eyes at the darkening woods and lifted his chin into the air, inhaling deeply. There was another monster in his forest. He got a whiff of fur before it disappeared on the wind. A clever monster, clearly, because he was on the move, staying downwind, and out of sight. He recognized the scent but couldn't place it. This werewolf wasn't a Bone-Ripper, but something else. Something bad. A creature with bad intentions.

The Taker was hungry, but not for Ashlyn as he'd expected. The Taker was hungry for any threat to her.

Huh.

He strode for the tree line, but he could feel it

now—the retreat of the beast. The darkness was leaving the woods of Winter's Edge. Asher was tempted to kneel in the snow and give his mind to the sky, use his powers to search for the wolf. To identify it. To devour it. But for some reason, he couldn't drag his consciousness away from the pretty little brunette currently laughing with the girls in Winter's Edge. All his wolf wanted to do was stay here, check parameters, make sure Ashlyn had fun with Mila and Blaire, make sure she was safe.

Clearly, Ashlyn had broken him. A snarl rattled his throat as his inner wolf disagreed. *She's not breaking you. She's shaping you into something different. A different kind of monster. One who can do good and bad.*

He should go talk to Odine. She hadn't seen Ashlyn in his future. She'd seen nothing but darkness, which didn't make sense because Ashlyn was as bright as the damn north star in an all-black sky. Surely Odine would've been able to see her if she was meant for him. She'd seen Blaire and Mila for his brothers.

Fury washed through him at the unfairness. Why was his future the only one shrouded in darkness?

When snowflakes drifted down from the sky, he lifted his face to the clouds. These were his favorite nights—the cold ones with a storm hovering above him, blotting out the stars and the moon. Blotting out the light. He liked the dark, frigid nights best when he went wolf, too. At least Odine had done that right. She'd given him a wolf that matched the rest of him. The rest of her decisions had put a canyon between her and Asher. Between her and anyone on this earth really, but sometimes Asher wondered if she even realized the consequences. Or perhaps she did understand, just preferred to be alone. He understood that desire.

Haunted souls did best in the confines of their hosts. Relationships with people required giving bits and pieces of them away to them for safekeeping, but Asher had learned long ago that in place of his soul was The Taker. And who, on this wide earth, would ever want to protect that?

Asher's wicked soul was his burden, and his burden alone.

He'd always been okay with that…until now. His boots crunched in the snow as he approached the window. His breath fogged in front of him on every exhale, so he held it in when he saw Ashlyn through the window pane, just so it wouldn't obstruct his view of her.

Beautiful face. Brave face. She was smiling and laughing, but her eyes didn't hide the sadness. She was hurt by Blaire's life here. Another lonely soul who had made the mistake of letting someone in, depending on them for happiness, and now look what happened—sadness in her eyes.

He watched her. That's what Asher did—he was an observer. He watched her when she didn't even know he was around. She wore every emotion on her face and made it easy to read her thoughts. Sure, he could read wisps of thoughts anyway. An empath, Odine called him, but it was more. He could sense more than emotional states. Sometimes he got words or phrases. If he listened hard enough, he could hear thoughts from people he knew. Strangers were harder, but lately, he could pluck thoughts right from Gentry and Roman, Mila and Blaire. And right now, as he reached for Ashlyn.

Asher.

She'd thought his name, so he allowed his lips to curve into a wicked smile.

ASHER

Asher confuses me. Stop thinking about him. You'll drop the bottle. Drop the bottle. You'll drop the bottle. Ashlyn spun an empty whiskey bottle like Mila was showing her and Blaire. *He kisses too rough. I always hated rough until Asher. Until him. Him. Until Asher. I like bad boys who are gentle, but Asher isn't gentle at all. Stop thinking about him. Focus.*

At least he wasn't alone in this. Her head was spinning around him, too, like he was the eye of the tornado and she'd been swept up. He had been swept up right along with her, and she was the eye of his storm.

He's a runner. Dad used to do that when things got hard. Run, run, maybe he would come back, maybe he wouldn't. Focus. Shit! The sound of shattering glass shook him from her mind. This wasn't right, being inside her head like this. He'd not only heard the words, he'd also gotten flashes of her dad—thick beard, young face, strong body. Her father had morphed in moments, older and more haggard with each frame. His beard had grown gray, and his body had shrunk until he looked emaciated. His eyes had dulled, his face sagged, his skin leathered, and in his hand had flashed a hundred drinks, one right after the other.

Asher frowned as Ashlyn bent down behind the bar. No wonder she didn't let people in easily. No wonder Blaire's absence hurt Ashlyn, but it wasn't Blaire's fault. She was a wolf now and had to hide it from Ashlyn for always. She couldn't go back home. Her place was here with Gentry. But the white wolf inside of Blaire didn't just hurt her. The wolf hurt Ashlyn, too.

He shouldn't be stealing thoughts from her. It wasn't right. She hadn't meant to show him her dad. Asher was a thief. Normally that wouldn't bother him. It never had before, but this woman was different. He wanted her to give him things willingly, not take them without her permission.

Ouch.

A wave of pain sliced across his palm, and Asher lifted his hand. There was a red, angry line, as if he'd cut it.

Inside, Ashlyn stood quickly behind the bar and stared at her hand. Crimson streamed down her palm.

Asher jerked away from the window and leaned his back against the wall of Winter's Edge, squeezing his right hand to ease the burning of the cut. What the fuck was happening? He shouldn't be linked to her like this!

Asher slammed down a wall between them, cutting himself off from her mind completely. Dizziness rolled through his head for a moment, and he swayed on his feet before he steadied out. He could smell blood. Her blood? The snow beside him was splattered with red that streamed from his fist. Shit.

He should go. He should hide this. Why did he feel ashamed? Fuck. Asher strode for the trail that would lead back to the inn, but his legs locked, and the wolf inside of him snarled long and low.

She was hurt. Asher stood there, chest heaving for three breaths before he spun and strode into Winter's Edge.

"Girls only," Blaire teased as he made his way behind the bar.

She and Mila giggled, but Ashlyn was clutching her hand to her stomach, holding a washrag. Clearly she hadn't told the girls she'd cut herself.

Asher felt insane right now. The need to fix her was making him shaky. The first-aid kit was under the cash register, so he yanked it out, looked at Ashlyn, twitched his head toward the kitchen, and walked through the door, praying to whatever power there was that she would follow him. If she didn't, he would carry her, and she would fight, because that's how his woman was. She fought. Fought him, fought change, fought everything, even if she did it with a smile on her face and a ready joke on her lips. He fucking loved that about her, but right now, his control was slipping.

Ashlyn shoved the swinging kitchen door open. She looked pale as she held her hand gingerly to her middle. Her eyes were a clear blue when she asked, "How did you know?"

"I watch you."

"Creepy."

"Watching is what I do."

"For your job."

He wasn't good at games, or dancing around questions. Asher didn't feel the need to talk much, but when he did, he liked to say exactly what he meant. "No, I watch you. I like to make sure you're okay."

That drew her up short. Her pretty lips parted like she wanted to say something, but nothing came out. A tiny thrill of victory zinged through him that he'd stunned her into silence for once, but it was short lived when he saw how red the washrag was getting.

Asher had always been steady under pressure, but right now, his heart was pounding, and panic seized him. She was hurt. Ashlyn was hurting, but he could make it all go away.

"I'm going to fix you," he whispered, already knowing he was about to make a huge mistake, but unable to stop himself. "Don't be scared."

****

Asher's eyes were such a strange color of blue right now; they almost looked silver in the fluorescent lighting of the kitchen. His face was twisted into something animal-like, his teeth gritted so hard the muscles in his jaw jumped as he trapped her with that otherworldly gaze. His body was humming with power she didn't understand and had never witnessed before in her life. He led her by the hand through a hallway beside the walk-in freezer. He pulled her into the dark of a room, but didn't bother turning on the lights of some sort of office before he shut the door gently closed behind them.

His eyes glowed strangely.

He'd told her not to be scared, and she wasn't...but she should be.

The first-aid kit clattered on the tile floor, and Asher brushed his fingertips down the outsides of her arms so gently her breath caught in her chest. Down, down he trailed his touch until he reached her wrists. He plucked the washrag from her fist, and she winced at the sting. It would need stitches. She'd been so careless, wasn't paying attention, and now look. It would take weeks to be able to properly use her hand again.

Warmth trickled down her fingers, but Asher intertwined his hands with hers. The burn lessened as he lifted her hands above her head and pressed her back against the door. And then he stunned her into stillness when he kissed her. His lips were soft against hers, shockingly so for a rough man like Asher. Her hand was tingling, but it wasn't painful like she'd expected. He squeezed her hand harder, but still, there was no pain...just that strange prickling sensation, as though she'd slept on her arm wrong and it had fallen asleep.

Asher angled his head the other way and eased

his tongue past her lips. He was pressed against her body, but he didn't trap her like his kiss earlier. This was different. The tingling stretched from her palm down her arm and into her chest, and though clothes separated them, she could feel his skin. It didn't make sense. Here in the dark, they were becoming one, and her mind was numbing, dulling. Asher was a spider who had given her a soft bite, injected her with something that was putting her to sleep. This was happy death. A soft, helpless moan came from her lips as she kissed him back. He pulled her free arm around his neck and swayed with her, dancing perhaps to the heavy silence. Something was coming from his skin. It felt strange against hers, like a warm breeze. When Ashlyn eased her eyes open, their clasped hands were glowing slightly. Behind Asher stood a dozen transparent figures.

Ashlyn gasped and pulled away from the kiss. The second her lips disengaged, the figures disappeared, and the mist from Asher's body evaporated.

"It's okay," he whispered, resting his forehead on hers. "They won't hurt you. They can't. I keep them from having any power."

"Asher," she squeaked, fear trilling through her.

"Are they ghosts?"

"Shhhh," he hushed her as he massaged the back of her neck and pulled her into a hug. "I won't let anything happen to you. Look, we're alone." Asher reached behind her and flipped on the light switch.

The sudden brightness hurt her eyes, and she winced. Her eyes adjusted, and she scanned the room. Indeed, they were alone.

Ashlyn looked at their hands, but they weren't glowing anymore. Had she imagined it?

Asher loosened his grip on her and turned her palm over for her to see. Ashlyn gasped. There was no cut, no mark, no blood at all. Her hand looked like she'd never touched the broken glass in the first place. But Asher's hand looked mangled. His entire palm was shredded. Blood welled up in the cuts, but not before she saw how deep and painful looking they were.

"What did you do?" she murmured, cupping his hand in hers as gently as she could.

Asher lifted his chin higher, his face completely passive. "I told you I was going to fix you."

Ashlyn jerked away from him and pressed herself against the door. No, no, no, this wasn't right. Asher had what? Taken her cut from her and put it on himself? Ghosts...glowing hands, glowing eyes...fuck. "What are you?"

His lip snarled up, and for an instant he looked like an animal. Not a sweet animal either, but a predator. "I'm whatever I have to be."

"Tell me you aren't evil," she whispered.

Hurt flashed across his face, and he ripped his silver gaze from her, gave it to the desk against the wall. "You can run now."

With a deep frown, Ashlyn reached for him, but Asher angled his body away from her, his eyes lightening even more. He swayed on his feet. "Run now, Ash. I'm hungry."

The way he said the last part lifted gooseflesh on her skin. There was warning in his words.

Push and pull. Asher was a professional at confusing her. She looked down at the bloody washrag, then from the discarded first aid kit to her smooth palm again. She ran her thumb along the place she'd been cut, but her skin didn't even tingle anymore. His hand, however, ran a river of red onto the white tile.

"Thank you," she whispered.

She wanted to wrap his hand and ease his hurt like he'd done for her, but Asher didn't want that, so she opened the door and left him there. The kitchen lights were on as she walked down the hallway, beckoning her with a welcoming glow. Behind her, she could tell the exact second Asher turned off the office light.

He really did prefer the dark.

It should scare her to give him her back as she heeded his warning and retreated from him, but it didn't. Her mind raced around what had just happened, but the terror that should've seized her left her alone.

Whatever he'd done to heal her, it had hurt him to do it.

A creature of darkness Asher may be, but evil he was not.

NINE

This was the part where she was supposed to run. In every scary movie she'd ever seen, there was a scene where the ditzy heroine could've saved herself, but chose not to listen to her instincts.

Was that Ashlyn's moment now?

She was freaking out. Shaking hands, sweating, panic flaring in her chest, racing heart. Her head said "flee and save yourself," while her heart said "weather the storm." Blaire was here, caught up in something Ashlyn didn't understand. Asher was here, sitting on the throne of her confusion. *Run now, Ash. I'm hungry.*

Hungry for what? Okay, she liked scary movies, and she was no ditz. She also read paranormal romances for the publisher she worked for! He was some kind of wizard or warlock, and healing her had made him hungry. Hopefully for steak since she was not a fan of having been finger-banged by a cannibal.

Run now.

She'd waved to Mila and Blaire and walked out of Winter's Edge with a sense of calm that had dissipated completely the second she stepped outside and away from his reserved demeanor. The panic set in as she'd speed-walked through the woods, probably teaming with ghosts because, apparently, those were real. She'd always believed in ghosts, but physically seeing them was a whole new beast to emotionally deal with. She'd ended up running the last hundred yards. Kind of. She'd never been super-athletic and was wearing snow boots with a heel, and she could've probably walked as fast as she ran. Then more freaking-out happened when she stepped in 1010 and immediately felt a chill on her skin. Asher had told her there was a ghost in here the day she'd arrived. The memory lifted chills all over her body and got her butt bookin' it to the bedroom to pack.

A wizard! A ghost-seeing, dark-loving, cut-healing wizard.

No wonder Blaire and Mila had warned her off him. They *knew*.

Ashlyn sat on top of the suitcase she'd thrown everything into and zipped it quick, then dragged it into the hallway and muscled it down the stairs.

She stopped at the door when she heard the soft murmur of voices. As quiet as she could, she set down her luggage and looked out the front window, but no one was there, just the dark porch and the parking lot with her car out front. Confused on where the sound was coming from, she padded to the back door and listened intently.

Yep, there it was—voices. Blaire's and occasionally Asher's. Being the curious little kitty she was, Ashlyn moseyed on over to the window and brushed the curtain gently aside with the very tip of her finger.

This didn't make sense, though. Asher and Blaire were indeed talking, but they were far away, all the way across the clearing of the back yard, nearly to the tree line. Ashlyn shouldn't have been able to hear them at all. Hell, she shouldn't be able to see them this well in the dark.

What was happening to her?

"You'll be the one to get us all busted, Asher," Blaire murmured. She looked angry, arms crossed over her chest, eyes blazing brightly. "Ashlyn is here for a week. Just...stay away from her."

Asher turned, pulled off his winter hat, and threw it at a tree. He rounded on Blaire. "I can't stop thinking about her. Can't stop following her. The wolf—"

"Needs to be controlled, Asher! She can't know about what's happened! You know the rules. You know the consequences. God, Asher, please tell me you understand the consequences! I died! I died for those rules. Your father died for those rules. Ashlyn deserves a normal, happy life. I love her, and you're going to kill her."

"I won't."

Blaire shook her head, looking more furious than Ashlyn had ever seen her. "She isn't some dumb human, Asher. She's smart. Sooo smart, and your eyes are the color of the moon right now. Do you even have control anymore? Hmmm?" Blaire arched her ruddy eyebrows. "Do you?"

Asher squatted down in the snow and looked at the cabin. When he looked right at Ashlyn, she stood by the window, frozen in his icy gaze. She couldn't drop the curtain even if she tried.

He sighed and shook his head. "If you want me to stay away, one of us has to leave. Ashlyn or me. If we both stay here, I'll want to be near her."

"Asher, she isn't for you. Her life is easy, void of pain, and without darkness. I want it to stay that way."

"And you think I don't? You think I don't know what I am, Blaire? You don't think I know what I'll do to a woman? You think I want to hurt her? I'd rather cut out my own fucking heart. I'm trying!"

"It's not enough."

Asher stood gracefully and strode toward the cabin. His eyes were almost white as the snow he walked across.

"Asher!" Blaire barked out.

"You win. I'll leave in the morning, but I'm pissed and I'm hungry, and I want to fucking drain you right now for making me go. No more bitching at me tonight, White Wolf. You'll stir up my demons."

Crap, oh crap, oh crap. Asher was coming in fast! Ashlyn bolted for the stairs but only got halfway up before the back door opened.

She froze like a deer in headlights, one hand on the railing, one leg bent and up on the next stair. She scrunched up her face and dared a look at him. Only he wasn't looking at her, but at her suitcase by the front door.

"It's icy out," he rumbled.

"You told me to run."

Asher scrubbed his hand down the blond beard on his face and heaved a sigh, closing his eyes when he did. When he opened them again and leveled her with a look, they were back to their normal frosty blue.

"Sooo…you're a wizard. I mean, you're a sexy wizard, but you can do magic tricks."

His eyes tightened to thin blue slits, and he pursed his mouth into a line. No answer. Great.

"You don't have to leave," Ashlyn told him. "I'll go. This is your home."

"I don't have a home. I have places I sleep."

Ashlyn turned, sat carefully on the stairs, and stared through the railing at him. "That's sad."

"To you. I'm happy with it."

"Are you happy, Asher? I rarely see you smile."

That seemed to draw him up short because he

straightened his spine and angled his head like a confused animal. "Smiles don't equal happiness to everyone."

"To humans, they do." She was fishing, hoping he would take the bait and let her in a little.

His lips twisted into a wicked smile, but he changed the subject. "Would you like to see my hand?"

"I don't like the sight of—"

He lifted a perfectly smooth palm.

"Blood," she finished quietly.

"Something about you makes me want to be reckless. I'm not careful enough around you. I want to show you things about myself just to watch your reactions. You confuse me. I've never wanted to shock anyone before. I like hiding, but with you, I get careless, and then I get this sick satisfaction when you don't run away screaming." His eyes flickered to the suitcase again. "Tonight was too much for you."

"Yeah."

"Before you leave, I want to take you to meet someone."

"You mean you want to drive me into the woods and chop me up? No thanks. I have better survival instincts than that," she teased.

He chuckled, and his smile reached his eyes now. And oh, Asher was stunning when he smiled. "Odine is someone important to me. Someone I don't share. I want her to lay eyes on you, and witness her reaction."

"Oh, so you're giving me something big then?" Ashlyn asked softly.

Asher dipped his chin once. "Meet her, and then I'll never bother you again. Meet her, and you'll understand me better. Meet her, and I can feel okay about letting you go."

"I won't tell a soul about anything that happened here."

"That's not what I mean about letting you go, Ashlyn."

She swallowed hard. She should stop asking for answers now because he was putting her fears at ease again, making her weak and vulnerable. But then again, she had to know. "What exactly do you mean?"

Asher arched an eyebrow as honesty pooled in his bright blue eyes. "I want to keep you. Something selfish inside of me wants you to stay here, so I can look at you, touch you, get to know you, and take care of you. You don't deserve that, though."

The last sentence hurt. "What do I deserve?"

"Better, Ashlyn. You deserve better."

"You say that like you mean it, but you want me to stay another night, and you want me to meet someone important to you."

Asher's smile dipped from his face as he approached the stairs. He climbed slowly toward Ashlyn. When he made it to her, he gripped her waist with one hand, brushed the side of his body against hers, and lowered his lips to her ear. "Because I told you...I'm selfish." He plucked at her sensitive earlobe with his lips so seductively she huffed a breath and rolled her eyes closed, gripping onto his shirt with her closed fist.

Bum-bum, bum-bum. A loud, quickening drum sound filled the stairwell. Was that...? Was that what she thought it was?

"I can hear your heartbeat," she whispered in awe.

Asher eased back, but the wickedness in his smile had turned to a worried frown. "What else do you hear?"

She gripped on tighter to his shirt and listened

hard. "The wind outside. The creaking of the trees. The woods here aren't silent like I thought. You breathing, me breathing, both of our hearts racing, a branch is scratching against a window, the hum of the refrigerator, electricity moving through the walls—"

"Stop."

Ashlyn opened her eyes, expecting the spell to be broken, but Asher was close, his lips only inches away from hers, his eyes intent on hers. He stood at an angle, as if his body was ready to pounce, muscles straining against his sweater, Adam's apple dipping with his deep swallow. "What if I'm not a wizard," he whispered. "What if I'm worse?"

"What if you're not as bad as you think?" she countered.

A soft rumbling sound emanated from his chest, and that sexy smile was back. So low she almost couldn't hear him, he murmured, "You have your eyes open, but you don't see me."

"What if I'm the only one who sees you?"

Asher's lips crashed onto hers, and his grip on her waist tightened. He was rough again, thrusting his tongue against hers, but this time she didn't want to punish him. She wanted him to be himself. His wild, chaotic, dominant self. Because Asher wasn't made in the mold of a normal man. He was made messy, and trying to clean him up, fix him, would strip away the things she was intrigued by.

Ashlyn slid her hands up his chest and then hugged his neck tight. He lifted her off the stairs and pulled her knees up until she was wrapped around him. And God, his erection was right there, pressing against the thin material of her leggings. Before she knew what was happening, her back was against the floor at the top of the stairs. How had he gotten her here so fast? Her stomach hadn't even had time to react, but a part of her loved that. More slipping, more recklessness, more exposing his power. More letting her in.

She shouldn't, but she trusted him. Sure, he probably had the potential to hurt people, but she'd only seen him heal. Sexy Asher, grinding against her hips, trailing biting kisses down her throat, but careful his teeth never broke the skin. Sexy Asher who was quiet with a poker face he only broke into a smile for her. Sexy Asher, yanking off her boots because he was done playing around. This was gasoline and a match, and she didn't want to extinguish the flame. If she was leaving tomorrow, she wanted to burn up with Asher tonight. And oh, this man was on fire.

He pulled his shirt from over his head and shoved it behind him on the stairs, his eight-pack flexing with the movement. She ran her fingertips up his stomach to his chest, memorizing the strength of his body as she went.

"Need to feel your skin," he growled in a voice that should've terrified her, but revved her up harder instead. Asher slid his hands up her sides, dragging her sweater with them, then pulled the fabric from her head and dropped it on the pile he'd started on the stairs behind him. His hands were steady, his eyes always on her as he lifted her easily and unsnapped her bra. This was the part of first-time sex she usually hated—the part where a new man would see her body. The part where her insecurities would rear their ugly heads and she would either ask for the lights to be turned off, or fight the urge to ask. But with Asher, it was different.

"Too loud," he murmured. Asher trailed his lips down her chest and drew a nipple into his mouth hard, making her hiss and arch her back. Rough man.

"What's too loud?" she asked.

"In your head. Shhhh, just be with me."

In her head?

He grunted and lifted his hand, and when he flicked his fingers, the lights blew in the house, raining sparks.

"What did you do?" she asked in shock.

"You wanted the lights off. Won't matter, though. I can see you just as well."

He could see her just as…? Ashlyn gasped. She could see him, too. There was no light in the house, but she could see him as if there were a full moon right over him.

"What's happening?" she asked.

Asher pulled her leggings down, down until they tickled her ankles, and he ripped them off. "I'm corrupting you, Sparkles." He didn't sound sorry at all.

Her body was on fire from his touch. Every nerve ending was exploding with pleasure where he massaged her breast, then slid his hand along her skin and gripped her hips. His lips were urgent as he kissed down to her stomach.

No man had ever made her feel like this before—

so drunk, numb, and sensitive just with the way he looked at her, touched her, and craved her.

All she could do was lay back and watch him move, watch him adore her body, watch him lose himself completely. Asher shoved her knees farther apart. Her instinct was usually to clamp them closed, but with him, she didn't want to. She wanted him to see everything about her, too. She wanted to let him in as repayment for showing her what he could do.

"Asher," she moaned, gripping his hair when his lips touched her inner thigh. Teaser, and she wanted him to stay aggressive right now. She gripped his hair harder and guided him. There was that sexy sound in his throat again—the one that said he was part monster. Her monster, and her monster wouldn't hurt her. He would keep her safe.

Asher gripped her hips so hard his fingers dug into her skin as he pushed his tongue into her. God, it felt so good to have part of him inside her. Ashlyn threw her head back and cried out as he slid into her again. Rocking her hips, she showed him how she liked it, and he responded perfectly, easing her into a good rhythm that was pushing her closer to release so fast, all she could do was ride the waves he created.

She was close, so close, moving with him. There. "Oooh," she moaned as her body shattered.

The snap of Asher's jeans popped, and she thought he would take her right away. Thought he would drive deep into her and feel her throbbing release for himself. His body was still humming with tension, every muscle rigid as he crawled up her body. But when he kissed her, something was different. He'd softened.

Asher sipped at her lips gently, plucking at them and only brushing his tongue shallowly into her mouth on every third kiss. He ran his knuckles down her ribs, down the curve of her waist, and around the swell of her hips. He opened his hand and ran his palm down the outside of her arm to her hand and intertwined their fingers, but still, he didn't lower his hips to hers. The fire inside of her calmed along with her fading aftershocks, but was replaced by something more. He was building up her need for him again, but the edge of desperation wasn't there anymore. Now, he was adoring her, and as he pulled her hand to his chest and pressed the flat of her palm onto the crease between his hard pecs, she realized he was asking her to adore him, too.

For some reason, it made her eyes prickle with tears. He was so different than what she'd expected. Dark Asher had a soft side that he likely exposed to no one. No one but her.

"Come here," he murmured against her lips, and then eased off her and sat back against the wall. Ashlyn hesitated for a moment. In this strange, dim lighting, his eyes reflected oddly, but his expression was soft.

Overcome by deep affection for him, Ashlyn crawled to him and straddled his lap. She cupped his cheeks and let his beard rasp against the palms of her hands before she slipped her arms around his shoulders and hugged him.

Asher let off a shuddering breath and slid his hands up her back. And then he held her, rocked her gently from side to side, and buried his face against her neck. Sure, his erection was still rigid against her sex, but he wasn't moving them for more right now. He seemed content to just be in her arms.

"I don't want to take you rough for our first time," he said, his voice low and gravelly.

"Okay," she murmured in surprise, blinking hard

at the wall and hugging him tighter.

Asher massaged the back of her neck, and ran his hand down her hair, tugging the ends over and over as he rocked them. It was cold in the cabin, in 1010, And when Ashlyn eased back to get a look at his face, his expression was relaxed, and he wore a slight smile.

"Sometimes you think too loud."

"Can you hear me?"

The smile dipped from his lips. "I try not to with you."

"Can you read minds?"

Asher shrugged one shoulder up and looked off down the stairs.

She was losing him, so she placed her palms on his cheeks and pulled his gaze back to her. "Can you?"

"I can do lots of things I didn't ask for."

"Do you want to talk about it?"

Asher shook his head slowly. "Talking doesn't help or make it go away, Ashlyn. It doesn't make me stronger or weaker, and it's not something I need."

"How do you know?"

Asher inhaled deeply and twirled his finger in the air beside her arm. "Can you see the blue?"

Ashlyn studied her arm, but it looked normal. "No."

"I crave you," he admitted low.

With a flattered smile, Ashlyn said, "I crave you, too."

The corner of Asher's lip lifted in the saddest smile. "Not like I do. We aren't the same."

Leaning into him, she asked in his ear, "What are you?"

Asher eased back and kissed her, then pulled away just enough to murmur, "Empath, perhaps." Kiss. "Incubus, perhaps." Kiss. "Darkness, definitely." Kiss. "The Taker." Kiss. The next one he closed his eyes when he whispered, "Wolf."

Only parts of that made sense, and she had a million questions, but she could feel the worry emanating from him. The shame. Desperate to make him okay again, to fix the sadness, she lifted off his lap, then slid over him slowly until he was buried deep inside of her.

Now it was Asher who arched his head back, eyes on her, but his groan sounded softly, and his eyes lightened. Tomorrow, when her head cleared, she would be afraid of all that was happening to Asher.

Scared for the power he managed. But tonight, she was going to love him and show him it was okay to be whatever he was. That he was enough for her.

Asher tensed as she rolled her hips against him, riding him slowly, hand gripping the back of his neck, eyes on his. She'd never been confident enough to do this with another man—take control—but for some reason, Asher felt safe. There was a heightened level of excitement being in the dominant position over a man like him.

Beautiful monster. My monster.

Asher's grip on her waist dug in harder, and his eyes blazed in the dark. She shouldn't be able to see him this well, but he was doing something strange to her body. He was sharing his power somehow. It wasn't scary. It was the ultimate let-in. A snarl rattled his throat, louder than he'd allowed before, so Ashlyn grinned at him. Good Asher, letting his control slip, but only for her. *Only me.*

"Only you," he ground out. He pushed off the wall and kissed her hard. Teeth knocked teeth, but it didn't hurt. It set her middle on fire as they moved together. Ocean waves. That's the only thing she could compare this to. Crashing ocean waves, and everything was getting louder, brighter. Too bright. Her chest felt strange against his. It vibrated, and she felt pulled closer to him.

And when she eased her eyes open, Asher was leaking black fog. It was thick, roiling from his skin, surrounding them. It had no scent, but it lifted her hair and caressed her skin. And that's when she saw the blue, entwining with the black, swirling like two tornados colliding. Her body hummed with power, but she couldn't stop moving against him. Asher's hand was gently gripping the back of her hair, and he was rocking against her, meeting each roll of her hips, and she was close. Soooo close.

"I won't hurt you," he promised, his eyes flickering to the storm that swirled around them. "I'll take care of you."

He was pushing so deeply into her now, his eyes intense as he gritted his teeth and watched her. His body was shaking. Asher was close, too, and she loved this. Loved being in the middle of this fucking volcano of power he'd created, yet still safe and warm against him.

For the first time since she'd met him, Asher wasn't running.

He was in this, right here with her, showing her his broken soul and asking her not to run either. Pressure built in her middle, and she cried out with every thrust as he pulled her down on his dick harder and harder.

He snarled and gripped the back of her neck, rested her forehead against his as she broke apart, her orgasm pulsing hard. Asher rammed into her and gritted out her name as he shot warmth into her. Over and over, he throbbed inside of her, filling her up until he huffed a shaky breath and pulled her tight against him. And as their aftershocks pounded on, he didn't move. He sat there frozen, holding her, breath quick, body tense.

The fog was receding back into him in thick plumes that looked like the aftermath of a burning house. He didn't grunt in pain or wince away. He just absorbed it, while she lifted her fingertips into the air and stared in awe at the cerulean blue that blanketed her skin. It was moving and transparent, like mist on an early morning.

"You know when you asked me my favorite color?" Asher said softly.

"Yeah."

"I've changed my mind."

She smiled at him. Already aware of his answer, she asked anyway. "What is your new favorite color?"

Asher flattened her palm, his eyes on the thin veil of blue that hovered above it. And suddenly, he touched the edge of the blue, then lifted his fingers away in a quick gesture. A wolf rose from the mist. Ashlyn's heart was in her throat as she watched the tiny figure running in place on her palm.

"Now, my favorite color is blue," he murmured.

The words didn't match, but Asher had just told her something incredibly important.

He'd just said, "I care for you deeply," in the only way he knew how.

TEN

"Do you come here often?" Ashlyn asked. "Spelled C-U-M." She giggled at her own joke.

Asher snorted and rolled his head toward her on the pillow, then pulled her closer against his side. "To ten-ten? Never. It's the first time I've been back to Rangeley at all since my dad disowned me."

With a frown, Ashlyn lifted her head and rested her chin on his chest. That sounded like an awful thing to go through. "He disowned you?"

Asher brushed her flyaway hair behind her ear and nodded. "Me and Roman both."

"Why?"

Her head rose with his ribcage as he inhaled deeply. Eyes on her hair as he stroked it back, he murmured, "I dated someone I shouldn't. So did my brother. It was against the rules, but I didn't agree with them."

"Did you love her?"

Asher nodded once. "I think so. She was the only before…"

"Before what?"

"Before you. Her name was Genevieve. I called her Gen. She wasn't scared of me. Lived a couple towns over with her dad and older brother. Her instincts were broken. They were too small. She would let me get away with things she should've questioned, and I thought that was love, so I took risks to be with her. My mom wasn't in my life, and my dad had chosen a favorite son in Gentry. I grew up different. Lonely. Quiet. I wanted someone to care about me, and it didn't really matter who it was. I just needed one person."

"And Genevieve was your person?"

Asher shook his head. "I made Gen sick the longer I was with her. Body sick and head sick. I couldn't stop myself from…"

"From what?"

Asher lifted his bright blue gaze to Ashlyn's. "I

couldn't stop feeding on her. I didn't have the control."

Ashlyn swallowed hard. "What do you mean feeding on her?"

"Gen's color was green."

Ashlyn looked at her hand where she'd seen the blue mist earlier. "What happened to her?"

"I tried to break it off when I saw how bad she was getting. I tried to stay away, but she would come to Rangeley, begging me to be with her, and I would give in every single time because I thought if she wanted to be with me despite the monster in me, then it really was love. I had such a craving for it. To feel cared about. To feel…anything. She got worse. Skinny, pale, sick to her stomach all the time, didn't have any energy to do the things she loved. Her dad was so worried. He asked me to leave her alone. He didn't know what I was, but he had some instinct that told him I was the one killing his daughter."

"How do you know?"

Asher tapped his temple with the tip of his finger. "I can hear people I know well. I was close to her father. I wished he was my dad most days. Her dad was scared of me at the end. So I broke it off for good.

I was determined because, if I didn't end it right then, I was going to kill her. Only she didn't stay away. She came to a meeting with my dad and his people, and she outed our relationship. And the next day, my dad disowned me and Roman both for shaming our family name. For shaming our people. For shaming ourselves."

"Just because of who she was?"

"No, Ashlyn. You should know everything. Not because of who Gen was, but because of *what* she was."

"What was she?" Ashlyn whispered, her blood chilled to ice.

"Human."

"Jesus," Ashlyn muttered, sitting up straight in the bed. She rubbed her hands rapidly up and down her arms to settle the gooseflesh there. "Asher, when you said you were all those things—incubus and empath and taker and wolf—you really meant you aren't human? What is The Taker? What does that mean?"

"It means I have something in me that takes life to live, Ashlyn."

"You're scaring me."

"You should be scared," he gritted out, sitting up.

"You should be screaming, sprinting for your car, leaving your goddamned luggage here in your rush to get away from me."

"Are you feeding on me?"

Asher reared back like he'd been slapped. "What?"

"Answer me. Are you feeding on me?"

"That's not the only—"

"Dammit, Asher. Just answer the question. Are. You. Feeding. On. Me?"

"I have."

Her eyes rimmed with tears, but she forced herself to hold his blazing gaze. "When?"

"Whenever you feel sick, that's me. That's The Taker."

She went over every moment since she'd come here. "So when you were with me in bed, and in the coffee shop?"

Asher made a tick sound behind his teeth and twitched his head. His eyes turned fiery in an instant, but he looked away. "The coffee shop was an accident. I was hurting Amanda, but you were too close. That wasn't for you. I haven't wanted to feed on you since I left your bed that first morning. I sat outside the door and gagged as I listened to the pained sounds you were making. And suddenly the blue that I thought would taste so good was like cement in my stomach. That was the moment."

"What moment?"

Asher tossed her a fiery glare. "That was the moment you became safe from me. The Taker shrank to nothing inside of me. It was the first time it felt shame. Regret. Remorse. It was the first time it thought of anything other than its own survival. That was the moment The Taker became The Giver, but only for you."

Ashlyn's eyes were leaking now, tears streaming down her cheeks as she curled in on herself and squeezed her hand into a fist—the one he'd taken the pain away from. "I'm supposed to leave tomorrow, remember? I'm supposed to leave, and you're saying all these things that make me want to stay and see everything you can do."

"Oh, you want to see how dark I can be?"

"No," she whispered around her tightening throat. "I want to see what kind of love you are capable of, Asher."

She'd never seen a man more stunned in her

entire life than Asher was right now. He sat frozen beside her, staring at her with wide, almost snow-white eyes, his blond brows lifted high.

"I don't fall easy," she admitted. "I never have. I don't like to attach to people, but for some reason, I feel safe attaching to you."

Asher shook his head in denial and warned, "Ashlyn—"

"No, let me finish before you try to convince me my instincts are broken like Genevieve's were. My eyes are open now, Asher. You've told me some of the real, and it's scary. Not for me, but I'm scared for all you shoulder. What a terrible burden on one man. But you've been doing it, and I fully believe these abilities were given to you because no one else would be strong enough to contain and control them. You're a monster, Asher, of that I'm certain." She lowered her voice to a whisper. "But you feel like my monster."

Asher's lips turned up into a wicked smile in the moment before his lips collided with hers. His kiss was explosive, firing from her lips down through her body one cell at a time, making her feel like she was glowing from the inside out. He ripped the covers off her lap and settled gracefully between the cradle of her thighs in a blur. So fast. So powerful. His hand was rough in the back of her hair as he pulled her face closer in desperation. And she got it. She was thirsty for him, too. When Asher slid into her, she cried out against his lips. God, he felt so good like this, taking her without hesitation. The gentle Asher from earlier was gone, and in his place was a rutting man as desperate as her to connect after those huge secrets had been exposed and left them both raw.

His abs flexed against her soft belly as he bucked into her harder and faster. *My monster.*

"Say it," he ground out, ramming into her again.

"My monster," she whispered through a naughty grin.

Asher rolled his eyes closed like those two words felt good, then pushed her knee back toward her ribcage and thrust into her deeper. Ashlyn lost her mind with how big and good he felt inside of her and dug her nails into his back.

"You better fucking make it count if you're gonna use your claws." Asher's voice was deep and gravelly, and there was a snarl in his chest that pushed her even closer to climax. Too fast. They were both on a collision course to Hell, but not tonight. Not right now. Right now, in this moment, everything was ecstasy, and the future seemed so far away.

Ashlyn dragged her nails down his back hard, and her man hissed softly behind his teeth and pushed into her faster. He lowered his chest to hers. Ashlyn cradled his head and then pulled his hair as he slammed into her again and again. His arms were so strong around her, so tight. There was no black fog, and no blue. It was just her and Asher here in the dark.

Her body shattered like broken mirror glass. She'd never felt anything like it. Sooo good, perfect, her orgasm blasted through her middle, gripping his dick in quick, pounding pulses. Asher pushed into her deep and froze. Warmth spilled into her, and then there were his teeth, right on her neck, gentle but sexy. Bitey...

Mate.

Bitey mate. Mate?

Yes, Ashlyn. Mine.

Asher?

I love, love you. I love you. Love. Fuck, you're so perfect. Beautiful. Brave girl. Love you.

She was so high on endorphins, she couldn't feel any fear right now. Asher was in her head. It didn't feel invasive. It felt intimate to share their release, their bodies, their minds.

And when their throbbing aftershocks had faded away, Asher let off a breath and kissed her gently. A couple nips on her lip, and then he rolled over, pulling her with him.

"You don't have to say it back," he murmured in the dark.

Ashlyn smiled and cuddled against her monster's chest.

"You want to know my new favorite color?" she asked softly, careful not to wreck the magic of the moment.

Asher kissed the top of her hair. "I want to know everything."

Ashlyn smiled and kissed the base of his throat. And for reasons she didn't understand, she bit him gently there.

When at last she eased away, Ashlyn whispered, "Now, my favorite color is black."

ELEVEN

Asher was standing out in the snow in front of the porch, blasting logs into bits for the fireplace. Tall as a tank, strong legs pressing against his jeans, his dark gray sweater lifting just enough to expose the bottom set of his abs every time he arced the ax back. Thick biceps flexing with every swing. Between swings, Asher couldn't seem to keep those sexy blue eyes off her. That, and he kept smiling to himself. She was tickled that he was obviously smitten with her, and also really turned on. Asher's smile was brighter than the sun. It took her breath away.

"Enjoying the view?" Asher grunted as he swung the ax down onto the log.

"Very much. This is fulfilling all of my pervy

lumberjack fantasies. I'll keep this locked in the vault for years." Ashlyn took a loud sip of her cherry cheesecake latte and looked at him primly as she pushed herself languidly on the swing with the toe of her boot.

He nudged a split log off the chopping block and replaced it with a new one. He'd gotten a whole tree from somewhere and dragged it up to the house, then taken a chainsaw to it in sections. Ashlyn didn't see a tractor or anything, so she assumed Asher also had super-cyborg strength, too. Sexy, because he was gentle with her, even though he could likely pop her like a water balloon.

Asher chuckled.

"Out of my head, mister!" she reprimanded him.

"A water balloon?"

Ashlyn thought hard about the grossest things she could think about. *Plain oatmeal, dung-beetles rolling up poop balls, smelly dumpsters, Butt-Grab Gary trying to kiss her with his mouth wide open in the broken elevator at work...*

"Okay, okay," Asher said, shaking his head. "I'm out." He bent and scooped up an armload of split logs like they weighed nothing.

It didn't look that hard, so Ashlyn set her drink down on the porch and threw the blanket off her lap, then pushed off the swing and made her way down the stairs. She filled her arms, but the wood was heavy, so it took her longer to settle it up on the pile where Asher was stacking the logs.

"You're so fucking cute," he said as he passed her. And to her surprise and delight, he kissed her hard and grabbed her ass, also hard. The devil was in his smile as he eased away and gave her a sexy-boy wink before he made his way back for another load.

Stunned by the unexpected affection, Ashlyn brushed the tip of her mittens against her lips. She loved the way he tasted and adored the way his lips always melted perfectly to hers.

"Asher?"

"Mmm?" he rumbled as he loaded his arms up again.

"Where did you get the latte? And the cinnamon rolls?"

The cup was the kind that could be purchased at the grocery store, so she'd thought perhaps he'd begged it off Blaire while Ashlyn was getting ready for the day.

"I went into town while you were in the shower. You deserve breakfast."

"Because I slept with you?"

He chuckled and made his way toward her with another armful of wood. "No, Ash. Because you're sweet, beautiful, and caring, and you make me feel different."

Swoon. Her legs wanted to buckle, but while he was being so open, she was going to pounce. "Feel different how?" she asked coyly.

Asher gave her a dark grin. "Like I don't want to kill everything."

"Mmm," she purred. "Romantic serial-killer poetry to my ears."

"Hey, you can still run."

Ashlyn looked down at her phone to check the time. "Hey look, my battery is at sixty-nine percent!"

"Favorite number?"

"Yep!"

"God, you're perfect."

"And you're a sappy romantic, mister. I didn't call that one."

Asher unloaded the wood to the pile and took a minute organizing it into neat rows before he turned to her and leaned back against it, arms crossed. "Only with you, Ashlyn. People are hard. I don't understand them because I've had to stay separate. I don't have a lot of experience with relationships. But with you..." He shrugged up one shoulder.

"But with me what?"

"You're easy."

"Thank you," she said, curtseying.

Asher rolled his eyes heavenward and then grinned at her. "Not like that, I'm not calling *you* easy."

"What if my new year's resolution was to be looser with men, and you just gave me a compliment, and then took it away?"

"Do you want me to feel bad?"

"Yes. Terrible. Maybe you should eat the rest of the pile of fifty cinnamon rolls before we go to your friend's house so you don't feel like feeding on me today. How many did you think I could eat?"

"I don't know. Maybe eight of them?"

"Eight?" she whisper-screamed. "They are the size of my head!"

"My people eat a lot. And the cinnamon rolls won't help. I could eat thirty of them. The human side of me would be full, but The Taker is a different part of me. It needs different food."

"Or you get sick?"

"Or I get weak, and I can't control myself."

"Well, that blows."

He snorted and hooked his hands on his hips, stared at the sky as he seemed to try and get ahold of his laughter. "You're so weird. None of this should be funny or okay with you. You should be freaking out."

Ashlyn lifted her sparkly pink rhinestone phone and shook it gently. "I have a freak-out penciled into my calendar for this afternoon. Prepare thyself. I will spiral hard."

"Will you cry?"

"Oh, *sob*. Just…curl up in a ball in the snow, and I'll wail phrases that don't make any sense like, 'I always pick bad boys, and this one eats everything and gives me tummy aches, but he's good with his hands, and blue-hoo-hooooo."

"Stop," Asher said, trying not to crack into a grin.

"If I pay you thirty dollars, will you come to my office and kiss me in front of Butt-Grab Gary and scare him away?"

"Gary will end up a dry gray corpse if you

introduce me to him. Still want to pay me to visit?"

"Kind of," she mumbled, texting Blaire she was about to leave for an adventure with Sexy Asher the Panty Basher. "Gary's really gross."

Asher lifted her off her feet so fast she squealed. In a rush, she ended up thrown over his massive shoulder, his hand smacking her ass so hard the sound echoed through the clearing.

"Asher! Fucker! You're going to leave a hand print!"

He nipped her side and chuckled remorselessly. Okay, from way up here, she was beginning to realize just how tall Asher was. And whooo, that butt looked good as he strode toward his truck parked in the middle of the parking lot. "How much do you weigh?"

"Isn't that rude to ask?" Asher muttered in an amused tone.

"For girls."

"How much do you weigh?"

She whispered her weight into his ear, and he laughed a booming sound, and said, "I weigh twice as much as you."

"Yeah, I could tell in the bedroom last night. I was almost a smear on the mattress after you finished with me."

Asher cracked up and oh, he had a great laugh. It was the deep, booming kind from low down in his belly that said he meant it when laughed at her jokes.

Blaire had texted back. Bouncing gently over his shoulder with the cadence of his gait, Ashlyn squinted her eyes and tried to focus enough to read it. Suddenly, Asher skidded to a stop, sliding slightly on the icy concrete.

Ashlyn twisted around to find Gentry, Roman, Mila, and Blaire standing near Asher's truck, dressed in warm clothes, and staring like she and Asher had turned into a pair of jumbo shrimps. Maybe her butt looked weird.

"Did I rip my pants?" she asked in a higher pitch than she'd intended.

"Uuuuh," Asher stumbled, setting her down quickly on her feet and then steadying her by placing her right in front of him and gripping her shoulders. "This is Ashlyn."

Roman narrowed his eyes. "Yeah, we know, dumbass. We've hung out with her."

More staring, and behind her, Asher's body was humming. Right. Ashlyn cleared her throat loudly.

"We like holding hands, and he thinks my jokes are funny."

"I don't understand," Gentry drawled out slowly.

Ashlyn sighed dramatically and spelled it out for them. "He's my monster. Any nay-sayers can fuck off. I like him."

"Oh, so you want to die," Roman said, nodding. "Awesome."

Blaire stuck up for her. "She's made her decision, she's a grown ass woman, she likes him, everything will probably be fine."

If she was closer, Ashlyn would've given her a high five, but at this distance, she scrunched up her face and nodded her head in a silent thank you Blaire would understand.

"Plus," Blaire continued, "I know Ashlyn. If you tell her no, she'll only hold onto him tighter."

"It's true," Ashlyn told Roman blandly. "I sink my claws in because I can't help myself."

"What are you doing out here?" Asher asked.

"We were all supposed to hang out today, remember?" Gentry arched his eyebrows high. "Pick up the liquor license for Winter's Edge and go out to lunch together. As a group. Family meal. Any of this ringing a bell? I texted you yesterday."

"I haven't checked my phone. I've been...occupied."

The way he said that last word made Ashlyn want to lean back against him and rub her butt against his crotch seductively. If she was a cat right now, she would be purring. She liked occupying Asher.

"We're going to meet Odine," Ashlyn explained. "Can we meet up for lunch after?"

Gentry offered her a slow blink, then lifted a pissed-off glare to Asher behind her. "Seriously?"

"You should come with us to see her," Asher said low.

"No thanks, we like survival," Roman uttered, draping an arm around Mila's shoulders and pulling her close to his side.

Behind Ashlyn, Asher sighed, and his grip tightened on her shoulders. "There's something you should know about her. Get in the truck."

Roman smiled and lifted his middle finger.

"Now," Asher said, but his voice was different. Gruffer and more demanding, and the effect on the others was instant. With jerky, uncoordinated movements, the others began to move toward the truck.

"Fuckin' Asherhole," Roman grumbled. But his middle finger didn't seem to be working anymore so he was just holding up a fist. "I call shotgun."

"Ashlyn gets shotgun," Asher said.

"I swear to God, Asher, if I have to see you two holding hands the whole way to Odine's, I'm going to barf."

Asher was gently guiding Ashlyn to the passenger's side door now as all four of the others scrambled into the back seat. "Payback's a bitch, Roman. I've watched all of you sucking face for weeks. If I have the urge to touch her, I'm going to do it."

Inside the truck, Roman looked disgusted. "Ew. Don't use the words 'urge' and 'do it' like that. It's weird."

"You say stupid shit all the time, and I don't call you out," Asher said.

He seemed to be waiting for Ashlyn to buckle, so she snapped it into place and gave him a big, bright grin. Then she puckered her lips like a fish and said, "Suck face with me."

Asher cast a quick glance to the seat behind her,

then licked his lips and pecked her quick. Roman made yacking sounds behind them, Mila giggled, Blaire said, "Aaaaw!" like she was watching a cheesy movie, and Gentry had apparently been shocked senseless because he wasn't even moving, just gawking with the biggest bright green eyes Ashlyn had ever seen.

She couldn't help the peel of giggles that burst out of her mouth as Asher shut the door and jogged around the front of the truck, scrubbing his hand down his face as he went.

Was he blushing? It was hard to tell behind his beard. Ashlyn hoped so.

The drive to Odine's was gently winding roads and snowy woods that looked like they belonged on a post card. "It's so beautiful here," she murmured to no one in particular.

"I'll never be used to it," Blaire said in an equally awed tone from where she sat on Gentry's lap in the back.

"I get tired of the snow sometimes," Mila admitted from where she sat in the middle seat between Roman and Gentry. "Sometimes I want to visit somewhere warm when it's like this."

"Fly south for the winter," Ashlyn murmured.

"Yeah. Not all winter, just…for a break." There was a frown in Mila's voice when she asked, "What are you doing?"

Ashlyn turned in her seat to see Roman typing on his phone. "Planning a vacation for us."

"Really?" Mila asked excitedly.

"Hell, yeah. Let's go to the ocean. I want to ravish you in a bathing suit."

"Dude, don't say 'ravish,'" Gentry muttered. "And wait on a vacation. We haven't even opened Winter's Edge yet, and Mila is our bar manager."

"Fuck off, Gentry. Mila's been trapped in Rangeley her whole life. If my lady wants a warm getaway, we're gonna go get buck wild, do it missionary-style on a public beach, and get sand in our cracks."

Mila bounced in the seat clapping as she chanted, "Sand in our cracks, sand in our cracks!"

"Pina coladas," Roman drawled. "Do you want a beach view?"

"Yes! Wait, how will this work with…you know…the Bone-Rippers?"

"Mila!" Gentry reprimanded her, then jerked his chin toward Ashlyn.

"Fuck the Bone-Rippers," Asher said, turning onto a one-lane road in the woods that was just a couple tire marks in the snow. "Mila deserves a break."

"Asher," Mila said, "maybe you should take them. You're scary enough to control them."

"Everyone stop talking! Rules!" Gentry gritted out.

"Says the guy who boinked a human," Roman muttered, still typing away on his phone.

Gentry looked pissed, buried his face against Blaire's back, and yelled against her shirt.

"Ashlyn, this is all a dream, and you won't remember any of this conversation tomorrow," Blaire said. But she was smiling. "I know you're the best with secrets. Ashlyn Michelle Jenkins, do you solemnly swear to keep everything you hear in this car and in this town a secret until you go to your grave, and then when you turn into a ghost, you have to keep the secrets from any ghost friends you make, too. Consequences—"

"Make 'em bad, Blaire, or I might slip up," Ashlyn said through a grin.

"If you spill a single secret, may your vagina stay as dry as the desert, and may you get an eyelash in your eyeball every single day for the rest of your life, and may wine taste like sewer water, and may you grow an allergy to cookies and pie and cake." Blaire stuck both pinkies out and canted her head, one delicate red eyebrow arched high.

Ashlyn pretended to think about it, but then squeaked in delight and hooked her pinkies with Blaire's. Together, they performed their synchronized weird handshake that they'd practiced for a month of lunches in the break room at work.

"Okay, Gentry. The pact is done," Blaire said. "It is now impossible for Ashlyn to tell a single soul."

When she looked at Asher, he was smiling and shaking his head, and easily, as if he'd been touching her his whole life, he slid his big hand over her thigh and squeezed her comfortingly.

"I like you," she said to him softly, because he should know how mushy he made her. "You don't have to say it back, though," she said, repeating his words from last night coyly as she turned up the radio like he sometimes did when he didn't want to talk.

"Ashlyn Michelle Jenkin's," Asher rumbled.

Whooo, it was sexy the way he said her full name.

She felt as drunk as a skunk after watching his lips curl around the words. Each syllable belonged to her, but Asher had just owned them. Whoa, she wanted to buck—and by buck, she meant fuck—right now.

"Yes?" she asked in a tiny voice.

"I like you, too."

Ashlyn's cheeks were on fire with pleasure as she threw her arms around her middle and stomped her feet to try and control the swarm of butterflies in her belly.

"Oh, my God, that was the cutest, sweetest thing I've ever heard from Asher!" Blaire exclaimed. "You two are so freaking cuuute!"

"Watch out!" Roman yelled suddenly.

Asher jerked his gaze back to the road and slammed on his breaks so hard the truck swung sideways and rocked to a stop.

Ashlyn didn't see anything, but Asher looked horrified as he stared out her window at the woods.

"Well, that's new," Gentry muttered.

"Does everyone else see the ravens?" Blaire asked in a small voice.

"Smells like black magic," Mila said so softly Ashlyn barely heard her. "Odine's been casting spells again in her woods. I see the ravens, too. Their eyes are bleeding, and the snow is soaked in red."

"Nope, not what I see," Roman said. "The woods are filled with ghosts, and I'm staring at Asher, age twenty right now. And the ghosts in these woods? They're all of us, Ashlyn included."

"That's what I see, too," Gentry said softly. "Is this real?"

Desperately, Ashlyn scanned the woods but saw nothing but a beautiful snowscape. "Show me," she whispered to Asher.

"Ash," he warned. "Some things are better left unseen."

"I told you already I want my eyes wide open on this. Show me."

Power hummed through his hand to her thigh, and her body tingled for a few moments before the scene before her transformed into one of horrors.

It was springtime, but there were no trees. They were all laid flat on the earth, dry with craggy branches. The sky was black with flocks of circling ravens, and in the middle of the clearing, Asher stood with his hands out, palms up, head thrown back, eyes closed to the sky. Black fog churned all around him.

The ground turned from green grasses and colorful wildflowers to silver ashes as the fog brought the sustenance back into Asher's body.

The graying landscape rotted away and stretched as far as the eye could see. He was eating everything up.

All around him stood transparent beings. Some, to her terror, she recognized. She and Blaire and Mila were holding hands, staring at Asher with haunted eyes. And Roman and Gentry stood just behind them, flanking them, looking sad. The rest were strangers, but they numbered in the hundreds.

"You wanted your eyes open on this," Asher murmured low. "Gentry asked if this was real. The ghosts are a product of what Odine has done to these woods. They aren't real, but what you see of me, devouring the earth…that is a memory, not a twisted figment of your imagination. It was real. I'd been hurt badly in a wolf fight with another rogue over territory. I needed the energy from other living things so that I could live. Ashlyn Michelle Jenkins…meet The Taker."

Chills blasted up her spine so hard and so fast her shoulders shook with them. Oh, she'd met The Taker last night. It had danced harmlessly with her blue mist, but it hadn't been intent on hurting her. And now, watching it ruin the earth made her aware of how dangerous he was.

But this was Asher. The one who had been quiet, respectful, watchful, and caring. The one who had bought her four dozen cinnamon rolls and a sweet drink he would've scoffed at just to make her happy. The one who touched her body and soul so gently he made her heart race and her breath quicken. The one who made her feel safe, even if he held great danger inside of him. The one who made her feel alive.

Ashlyn slid her hand into his and inhaled deeply as she looked at him. "Okay," she murmured.

"Ashlyn," Blaire said softly, as if she was weak and pitiful and didn't know what she was getting herself into.

Ashlyn held Asher's gaze when she said, "I wanted to know, and now I do. It's my choice whether to stay in this or not."

"And?" Asher asked.

"Take me to meet Odine."

TWELVE

Odine's home was a small cabin in the middle of the wilderness. Fresh snow covered the roof and the pile of firewood stacked along the front of the house. Curls of smoke spilled out of the stone chimney. The house would look downright cozy if not for the strange markings etched into the trees and the four bird skulls hanging from a post out front.

"So Odine is a..."

"Witch," Asher answered at the same time Gentry said, "demon," and Roman muttered, "psychopath."

"And how do you all know her?" Ashlyn asked as the truck rocked to a stop in the front yard.

"She was banging our dad before he died. Probably the reason he got killed," Roman said darkly. "Don't piss her off. That woman can break you with little effort."

Yikes. Wringing her hands, she let off a nervous laugh and scrunched up her face at Asher.

He chuckled and promised, "I'll keep you safe. My Taker is bigger and meaner than hers."

Asher shoved his door open and got out, but Roman piped up. "Wait, what does The Taker mean?"

"You'll see," Asher called as he shut the door behind him.

Ashlyn was halfway to slipping out of his big-ass truck and into the snow, but Asher appeared suddenly and grabbed her waist, steadying her.

"Gentleman," she accused.

"Gentlemonster," he corrected her.

"Hmmm," she hummed happily, sliding her arms around his waist. "I like that you don't hide from me."

Asher shrugged nonchalantly and massaged the back of her neck as he hugged her. "If you became overwhelmed, I would just take that memory."

"You better not mess with my memories ever, Asher. I would be pissed."

"But you wouldn't know to be pissed because you wouldn't remember why you were supposed to be pissed," Roman said as he stomped by. "Still want the fealty of a lunatic, Ashlyn? P. S. I fucking hate this place. It stinks like black magic and bad stuff happens here. Whose stupid idea was it to visit Psychodine when we were supposed to be eating fried chicken and gravy right now?" He tossed Asher a hate-filled look and muttered, "And I'm still mad that you forced us into the car. That alpha shit's messed up."

"Would you like it better if I bossed you around?" Mila asked, taking his hand as they walked toward the cabin.

"Yes, but that's different. You give me blow jobs."

"God, Roman," Blaire muttered from where she walked next to Gentry behind Ashlyn and Asher.

Ashlyn was trying to contain her smile, really she was, because meeting Odine had her a little scared right now, but the rapport of this group of smarmy weirdos was downright amusing. They were her kind of people.

The door to the cabin swung open, but no one was there. When it banged against the wall, Ashlyn jumped at the sound. Asher didn't allow her to hesitate, though. He pulled her by the hand up the steps and inside of the small home. It smelled bad.

Like herbs and the dried plants that hung in clusters from the exposed rafters on the ceiling, yes, but also like something had died in here.

"Lots of somethings," Asher murmured, casting her an emotionless glance.

She would never get used to him being in her head. Never.

"Then don't think so loudly, Ash. I'm trying to stay out."

"Am I missing something?" Roman asked. "There is a very one-sided conversation going on here, and I can see the ghosts, Asher. You aren't talkin' to them."

"Odine," Asher called, ignoring his brother.

"Down here," came a muffled answer.

Asher led them along a short hallway and down a set of rickety stairs into a basement. The walls were lined with aged books covered in dust. In the center of the room was a long table covered in plants, old books, disorganized piles of notes, dirt, animal skulls, and one brown rat, that crept among the mess, sniffing and twitching its whiskers.

Ashlyn wasn't a fan of rodents, so she kept carefully hidden behind Asher.

Dust motes swirled in the sunrays that streamed

through a small, soiled window near the top of the wall. When a woman stepped out of the shadows and into the sunrays, Ashlyn gasped. She was older, but beautiful, with dark eyes, olive-toned skin, and jet black hair streaked with silver. There was a familiarity to the set of her eyes. They slanted upward slightly, just like Asher's.

"You've brought them here to call me out," Odine murmured. She sounded unhappy as she leveled Asher with a glare.

"It's time."

"Maybe." Odine lifted a gnarled finger to Ashlyn. "It's never time for you to bring that one to me, though."

Asher slipped his hand around Ashlyn's and pulled her forward. "Have you seen her for me?"

Odine didn't answer, but instead her eyes sparked with a fire Ashlyn didn't understand. After a loaded minute, she admitted, "I have had visions for all my sons. Ashlyn is the one I didn't want. She's the one I'll do anything to stop."

"Wait," Gentry said, stepping forward from where he'd been leaning against the wall near Blaire. "Your sons?"

ASHER

Odine flicked her fingers and a book fell open on the table. A rectangle had been cut from the texts, and nestled inside was a stack of pictures.

Roman was closest and took the picture from the top of the pile, studied it for a moment, then muttered a curse and replaced it. He backed away, looking shocked, running his hands through his hair as Mila followed him, hands out. "Babe," she whispered.

"No way, no fuckin' way," Roman said, his eyes brimming with emotion. "We had a mother, and she died."

"Roman," Odine said in a breaking voice as she stepped closer.

"Don't you take another fucking step!"

Gentry was looking through the photos now, shaking his head. From his profile, Ashlyn could see the exact second a drop of water dripped from his chin. "You weren't there."

"I was always there."

"You weren't there!" Gentry yelled, rounding on her. "You weren't. When we needed a fucking mother, where were you? Why weren't you helping dad raise us? Why were you letting him favor me? Why were you letting him treat Asher and Roman like shit?

Where were you when they were kicked out of the pack? Where were you when I was left here all alone?"

Blaire was crying now, rubbing his back, right between his shoulder blades.

"I was human," Odine whispered. Her eyes were rimmed with tears that spilled over. "And not just human, but a witch. And I'd given awful powers to you boys when I had you. Your father and I could tell right away that you were tainted with my darkness. Asher most of all. I had to do something to give you a better life."

"A better life than one raised by our own mother?" Roman asked. His blazing blue eyes morphed to gold as a tear spilled onto his cheek. He twitched his face fast and wiped his cheek on his shoulder. "Do you know how hard it was growing up without you?"

"Yes!" Odine yelled. "I was suffering, too! But Asher would've been devoured by the darkness inside of him within two years. Roman, you and Gentry would've lasted longer, but not by much. I wanted a better life for you, so I gave you wolves, like your father had. And I gave him my blessing to take you into the bosom of a pack he created, one specifically made to support strong, dominant, troubled wolves, so you could be steady, control your powers, and have a goddamn shot at happiness. Because I love you three. More than anything! And that's all I ever wanted was for you to be happy. I'd ruined that by being your mother and giving you darkness. So I gave you the wolves to make you stronger, and I let you go, and it ripped my goddamn heart out every day to be separated from you, but I couldn't be a part of that pack with you. Because I'm fucking human, and as much as I tried, and God knows I tried, I couldn't raise a wolf within me." Odine's shoulders hunched and tears dripped from her chin. "I saw Mila for you, Roman, and so I kept her here, so you could be happy together. I watched her grow up from afar, and she felt like the daughter of my heart. I saw Blaire for you, Gentry, a white wolf, beautiful, pure, steady, kind, all the things you deserved, and so I waited for her to be ready, for you to be ready, and I brought her here knowing she would be bitten and I would have to raise her wolf. And I would do it again because I see you smile now. It's the same smile I adored when you were a boy, when you hugged me, or listened to my bedtime stories, or ran around the yard with your brothers."

"Why didn't you tell us?" Roman yelled.

"Because I just got you back! You didn't know you were half human. You didn't know you had witches peppered throughout your lineage. You weren't ready to hear it!"

"You saw Ashlyn," Asher said in a low snarl. "So you've been lying to me. All this time you said there was no one for me. That I was meant to be alone."

"You knew?" Roman yelled. "Fuck, Asher, seriously? You knew she was our mom?"

"Yes, and I couldn't tell you."

"Why not?" Gentry asked.

"Because I made a promise to Odine! I made a promise I couldn't break. She wasn't ready, and neither were you two. We were so deep in our hate for each other for so many years, Odine wasn't going to be the glue for us. She would scatter us to the wind even farther. I had dreams of her when I hit twenty. Memories of our mother. Of Odine. Good ones. Ones that made me yearn for understanding of myself and what happened here. So I returned to Rangeley, and I found her. And she helped me get some control over

The Taker."

"What the fuck is The Taker?" Gentry growled.

Ashlyn slid her hand up Asher's tense back, then hugged his side, because he was humming with power again, and this basement was too small for a man like him to lose control.

Asher let off a long, steadying breath. "The Taker is my darkness. It's the part of me that could destroy the world if I'm not perfectly in control all of the time."

"Holy shit," Roman muttered, pacing to the door and back.

"Explain Ashlyn," Asher gritted out to Odine.

With a slow blink, Odine lowered her onyx gaze to Ashlyn's. And in a voice void of emotion, she uttered, "Ashlyn will be responsible for your death."

"What?" Ashlyn whispered.

"Yours was the easiest future to read, Asher. Your fate was written in the stars from the moment I held you in my arms for the first time. Your death is soon, and you will die to protect a helpless human from an evil that has been building on the outskirts of Rangeley. You've felt it, son. Felt the wolf hunting you. Mila's waited too long to secure the Bone-

Rippers' loyalty. I see you as an alpha, Asher. It was always you. Your father knew my predictions, and so he went to work. He thought if we changed one thread on the spider web of your destiny, it would alter the makeup entirely. And so he raised Gentry to be alpha because he was convinced if Asher wasn't ever alpha, Fate would change its course. He put all his focus on pushing Gentry to take over the pack you were destined to rule because if he was alpha, you would never take it from him, and maybe, just maybe, you would live the long life we desperately wanted for you. Roman and Asher, you thought your father didn't love you, but that was never the case for even a moment. He was just trying to save the son he knew he would lose too soon. It was an obsession, saving Asher, and he died with so many regrets."

Roman and Asher slid emotion-filled gazes to the darkest corner of the room.

And then, so fast he blurred, Roman picked up an empty mason jar and chucked it at the wall right where they were staring. It exploded into a million tiny shards of glass. "You couldn't just fucking tell us why you didn't care about us? Huh? You couldn't explain you *had* to build Gentry up? Instead we had to feel worthless for always? For our whole fucking lives?"

"You should've told me you saw Ashlyn before," Asher growled in a voice that couldn't pass for human.

"And if I did? If I told you there was a mate out there for you? What would you have done? Even if you knew she would be the death of you, what would you have done, my lonely boy?"

Asher rested his back against the wall and scrubbed his hand down his beard, blazing silver eyes locked on Odine. He slid his attention to Ashlyn, and she could see the answer there before he even said it. "I would've found her earlier so I could have more time with her."

"Listen to me, Asher," Odine demanded. "I still see it so clearly. You will die in the snowy woods of Winter's Edge, while your brothers and their mates lie bloody in the snow near you. Ashlyn will survive because you will give your life for hers. Before that happens, she's going to fix you, Asher. She'll soak up your darkness and leave you weaponless against the storm that is hunting you."

"Then I'll leave," Ashlyn said in a shaky voice. "I'll

be the thread that changes. He can't give his life for me if I'm not here."

"But I don't want you to leave," Asher gritted out.

"Dude, she'll kill you," Roman said, hands on his hips as he glared at his older brother.

"I just got her, Roman! I like how I feel around her. I've had her a few days, that's all. Would you be fine with Mila going? Just cold turkey, cutting off from her, bye Mila? Hmm?" Asher canted his head and arched his blond eyebrows. "Would you?"

Roman wouldn't meet his eyes anymore, and instead looked down at the floorboards and shook his head. "No."

Hopeful, Ashlyn said, "Maybe the prediction won't come true."

Blaire looked at her with such sympathy in her green eyes. "Odine's predictions always come true."

"It's bullshit," Asher said, straightening his spine and pacing the back wall. "It's bullshit! Roman and Gentry get their happily ever after. They were on a collision course from birth, and what did I get? More power than I can manage, power that kept me separate, power that kept me alone, and now that I've found someone who makes me happy, and who eases that ache—and it's a fucking *ache*—I have to let her go? No."

"Asher," Mila whispered.

"No! You want to help, Mila? Go be alpha of the Bone-Rippers. Secure them under you. Bind them. It's your right, you killed Rhett, go take your place on that throne. I won't challenge you. I won't take the pack from you. I don't even want to be a fucking alpha. Until the day Ashlyn tires of me, I'm keeping her."

Asher grabbed Ashlyn's hand and led her up the basement stairs.

"And if she fixes The Taker?" Odine called after him.

"Good, I hope she does. I never wanted it anyway, *Mom*."

There was a humming inside of her chest. "Asher?" she asked softly as he tugged her faster up the stairs.

"I feel it, too."

So it wasn't his power rattling the house now. Shit! Terror pushed her legs faster as they bolted across the living room and out the front door. But the humming only got louder when they stepped outside, and when Ashlyn looked into the woods, she gasped. Odine stood there, raven-dark hair whipping in the wind as she held her hand out toward them, fingers clawed. There was a blue spark flickering over her palm.

"You'll see what he really is before you make this choice, Ashlyn," Odine said over the wind, which was kicking up by the moment.

"Odine, stop!" Asher roared, shoving Ashlyn behind him. There was still another fifteen yards until they reached the truck.

Odine flicked her fingers, and the truck slid sideways, the tires making deep rivets in the black earth under the snow. It rocked to a violent stop at the edge of the woods, and now Odine was yelling words that made no sense. They were guttural sounds and in a language Ashlyn hadn't a guess at.

"Oh, my gosh," Ashlyn whispered.

She turned to see Blaire running for her. She looked horrified, her cheeks flushed and her bright green eyes wide. "Ashlyn, run!"

A wall of snow shot straight into the air, blotting out Blaire and the others completely. Ashlyn looked down at her feet where all the snow was disappearing, being sucked into that barrier.

"Shit," Asher snarled, his head snapping to the side. "Ashlyn, back away." He dropped to his knees but it didn't look on purpose, his movements jerky. Black fog was leaking from his skin now in rivers of pitch darkness. His clothes were burning off with it and falling to the ground in wisps of gray ashes. Ashlyn bolted for the edge of the snow wall to run around it and escape, but Odine's voice grew louder, battling the roaring wind, and the barrier formed a closed circle, trapping Ashlyn inside the center with Asher and Odine.

She reached out and touched the snow, and it burned her finger like fire. With a cry, she yanked her hand back and looked in horror at the bleeding raw skin of her fingertips.

When Asher roared in pain, Ashlyn spun around to see his body breaking. That's all she could think to describe it. The snapping of a bone, and then another and another, echoed above the wind as the fog rolled out of him in thick waves. The snow was gone from the center of the circle, and now she could see the effects of The Taker. The darkness was scorching the earth around Asher's body. And it was slowly creeping her way.

"Don't do this," Asher begged, blazing white eyes on Odine. He was doubled over, and his face was twisted in agony as he fought something Ashlyn couldn't comprehend.

"She leaves or she dies," Odine said between chanting.

"You'll have me kill her? You'll have me kill my mate? Fuck!" Asher screamed, the veins in his neck straining as he pitched forward, his palms landing hard on the ground. "You'll have me kill you?" he asked in a strangled voice. "I'll choose her, Odine. The Taker will choose her, too. Let me up, or you'll breathe your last breath for this."

"I love you! You're my firstborn, my Asher Boy. It's you above her, you above me."

Ashlyn whimpered and sidestepped as tendrils of inky mist reached for her ankles. "I'll leave. I swear I'll leave, just let him up!"

"Behold the monster you've fallen in lust with, sweet Ashlyn," Odine called. She clenched her fist around the flickering blue flame and twisted her wrist. And in that moment, something horrible exploded from Asher. A black-furred monster with white eyes and razor sharp teeth. One whose coarse, dark hair spiked along his back as he rose from the fog, bigger and bigger until Ashlyn had to arch her neck back to take in the massive body of a beastly wolf.

The mist had reached her, and there was nowhere to go, nowhere to escape. There was a wall of burning snow behind her, and the circle was filled with The Taker.

Ashlyn doubled over the ripping pain in her stomach as the dark pulsed into her body. "Asher," she choked out.

Asher took his hate-filled gaze off Odine and slid those terrifying white eyes to Ashlyn. And instantly, the pain eased and the fog lifted and hovered just above her skin. Power pulsed from the wolf, and the snow wall blasted outward and disappeared completely. The darkness lifted into the air, concentrating until it wasn't transparent anymore, but was like black water, churning around the wolf.

Odine stopped her chanting and gasped in the instant before The Taker blasted into her. Blasted through her. Blasted through the woods, leveling every tree behind Odine.

He was going to kill his mother…for her.

"Asher stop!" she screamed, running for the witch, who was down on her knees in the black cloud.

Maybe Odine was dead already, Ashlyn didn't know. All she knew was she had to try and save her, not because she cared about her, but because, if Asher did this, his soul would be unsalvageable, and he would be lost forever.

From behind her, Blaire and the others were screaming something she couldn't understand, but she didn't slow down. She couldn't. Odine's breaths were severely numbered right now.

The second before she burst into the fog, she looked over her shoulder at Asher, and what she saw there scared her. His eyes were completely white and full of fury, focused on Odine. He didn't even react or look at Ashlyn. He was intent on the destruction of the woman who'd tried to hurt her. Asher was the gentlemonster no more.

Ashlyn burst into the fog, expecting immediate pain, but none came. Instead, only a throbbing, humming sensation of great power pulsed against her body as she slid on her knees in the cold dirt and tackled Odine. Ashlyn covered her with her body and

gritted her teeth. And then something happened to her. Something she didn't understand, or know how to control. A wave of energy pulsed out of her body. And she could see it, even without Asher touching her. She could see the blue, growing out from her skin, dancing with the black, mixing, swirling, creating a barrier over her and Odine's limp body.
Please be alive.

A chill-inducing howl lifted into the air, followed by a smattering of pops like gunfire. And then another howl joined, and another, and another, and another.

The Strikers were werewolves. Mother. Fucking. Werewolves. And included in that was Blaire. She approached through the mist, loping along the edge. She was white-furred and fanged, but her eyes were worried and locked on Ashlyn. There was her friend. There was her Blaire, just in a different body. This was why she was in Rangeley. This was why she'd never come home. Even if she wanted to, she couldn't.

Ashlyn cradled Odine to her chest. The woman was shaking, cold perhaps, but at least she was still alive.

The blue was growing and sparking like a storm cloud hiding lightning. It hurt now. Her skin tingled, and her body ached more by the second. Tears streamed down her cheeks as the colors mixed and turned in a slow-moving cyclone around them. The black was disappearing into her blue, darkening it. Darkening her. She was ripping apart, pulling the dark into her. No! That's not what she wanted. She wanted to stay separate.

Get out of there. It was Asher's voice in her head. *Ashlyn, let her go!*

But she couldn't. Her body was stuck to Odine, and the woman was staring up at her with wide, black eyes. "Don't hurt my son," Odine whispered.

But Ashlyn wasn't trying to hurt him. She was trying to save him. Save his soul from the dark. He wasn't like Odine. He wasn't made to be ruthless, or shoulder the burden of infinite power. Didn't Odine see how tired he was? Didn't she see the toll? Didn't she see Ashlyn's war was with The Taker right now, not with Asher? Didn't she see how much Ashlyn already loved him? Loved him? Yeah. That felt right. Perfectly right. Love.

With her body feeling like it was breaking apart,

Ashlyn looked over her shoulder at Asher, but he was drawing the dark blue fog back into himself, head down, tail lowered, eyes churning with pain. He was trying to protect her, but he was taking some of her with him. Ashlyn stumbled to her feet and swayed, locked her legs to stay upright.

"Enough," she murmured.

Asher ran for her, his massive black claws digging into the earth. Her legs gave way. Time slowed. In a burst of midnight blue fog, Asher changed into a man and caught her in his strong arms before she hit the ground.

Ashlyn felt a hundred years old. She felt like she hadn't slept in years. The exhaustion was bone-deep, but she didn't want to close her eyes yet. Not until she made sure he was still okay, still with her, still salvageable.

Asher searched her face with eyes that darkened from white to frost blue. "What did you do?"

"I saved your soul," she whispered. But she'd heard Odine's prediction, and now she'd created one of the threads in the spider web of his fate by warring with The Taker. "I saved your soul, and I killed you."

And before she closed her eyes and gave into the

exhaustion, she realized something heartbreaking.

She was going to have to leave him to save his life.

THIRTEEN

"You didn't cure me, Ashlyn." It was the first thing Asher had said to her since this morning. In fact, it was the first time he'd even looked at her. He'd driven her back to Hunter Cove Inn in silence, staring straight ahead like she didn't exist at all. And then, as soon as he dropped her and the others off, he drove away. He ran again.

And when he'd returned after being gone all day, he'd asked to talk to her here, in the bar his father had owned.

Ashlyn looked around Winter's Edge. The tavern was almost ready for the Grand Opening, all the permits were in, the liquor license secured, every dust mote had been evicted, every glass washed, every seat was ready for a patron. All that was left was to hang some old pictures Asher's dad used to have hanging on the walls, and put the Grand Opening sign over the door. "Tomorrow, we should have this place totally ready."

"I won't be here."

She dried the last shot glass and set it in the row with the others. At his admission, she huffed a soft laugh and shook her head. "You ever gonna stop—"

"I'm not running. Not this time. I'm hunting."

Ashlyn frowned and leaned her elbows on the bar as he took the stool on the other side. "Hunting what?"

"Evil."

"The wolf Odine said was after you?"

His eyes flashed silver as he nodded his head. "I can hear what you're thinking, Ashlyn. You're going to leave me." He looked sick as he said those last words.

"We just met—"

"Don't do that. It's such a human thing to say."

"Well, I'm human."

Asher gritted his teeth so hard his jaw worked under his blond whiskers. "The Taker is still there, still so fucking easy for me to reach, still hungry. Odine was wrong. You didn't fix that part of me. You just…changed it a little. I don't feel so…heavy. We need to talk about what you saw."

"The wolf?"

"Yeah." His Adam's apple bobbed as he swallowed hard. He rested his arms on the bar before he unscrewed the cap of a shaker and dumped a pile of salt onto the shining counter. And then he sketched a quick wolf with the tip of his finger.

"When you told me the things you are, I didn't pay attention to the wolf one. I thought it was a turn of phrase. I thought you meant you were a predator of some sort, not a real wolf. Asher…"

"I know. He's a lot to accept."

"All of this is."

"So is this the freak out you scheduled into your phone?" His silver eyes flashed to her. His lip was quirked up in the smallest smile, but it faded the second he saw her face, and then he dropped his attention back to the salt.

This wasn't a joke. This was life and death. His death.

"You disappeared on me today, and do you know

how I spent that time? With Blaire and Mila in tenten, crying my eyes out, hugging a pillow on the couch that smelled like you, staring into the fireplace while those two girls, those two *werewolves*, explained everything that's happened in Rangeley. And right inside the front door stood two Striker brothers who looked relaxed enough, but I wasn't fooled. Roman and Gentry were there to make sure I didn't leave. They were standing guard against me. And I get it. I'm human. I'm other. I'm a threat if I ever outed you or your people. I would never, but they don't know me well enough to trust me completely. Not like Blaire does. So I know everything now, Asher. Blaire made sure I wasn't left in the dark about anything. She told me what happened to her. She also told me if you bite me, I'll die."

"I would never bite you. Or feed on you, or hurt you at all. I can't anymore, Ashlyn. You belong to me. You belong to The Taker."

If any other man would've declared she belonged to them, she would've balked. She was independent, stubborn, and her own woman. But the way Asher had said it, with such devotion on his lips, she only fell deeper for him. "You know when something really good and really bad is happening at once? It's like I'm standing on this platform over nothing, and the bottom is crumbling away, and I'm rushing to learn how to fly. I'm scared, but just think if I pulled it off. Just think if I flew."

"Then fly, Ash. Stay here. Stay with me. Let me handle my own fate, let me fix it, let me protect both of us."

"But what if flying means losing you?" she asked in a small voice. "Things obviously work different for you—"

"We've bonded, yes."

"Asher, let me finish and stay out of my head so I can think for myself. Don't finish my thoughts right now."

He swallowed hard again and nodded once.

"I'm human, though, and afraid of how strongly I already feel for you. I feel like I've known you my whole life instead of a few days. It's not supposed to be like that—this strong, this fast. I've never had the urge to settle down with a single person, and then when I look at you...I see my whole future. It *revolves* around you, around this town, and I imagine Blaire and I raising little werewolf babies together in the same…I don't know…commune or pack, or however the inn works."

"I'm rogue, so no pack, and our children will be human."

"Will be? Asher, do you see that future, too?"

He shook his head. "I don't see it, but I want it. With you." He ran his hand down his beard and relaxed back in his seat, canted his head, leveled her with a look that made her heart skip a beat. "I've wanted one person for myself. One person who looks at me like I'm normal. Like I'm worth taking risks for. And I thought, after Genevieve, I would never have that because I would drain anyone who got close. But I don't drain you. I want to make you smile, and feel safe, and buy you shit. Ashlyn, I can't even walk by a goddamn store without thinking, 'Would she like that?' That includes the grocery store. I bought these damn frilly cupcakes because they had pink sparkly sprinkles on top. You asked me once if I was happy. You didn't think so because I never smile. But I wanted to see your face when you saw those cupcakes because your smile is my happiness. The thought of losing that after I've tasted the relief you've given my soul? I can't. I can't go back to the dark now. Please don't leave. Give me time to hunt whatever is hunting me. I'll end it outside of Winter's Edge woods and ruin Odine's prediction. I'll keep you safe."

"I don't care about me, Asher. It's *you*. I want *you* to be safe."

Asher shook his head, and his brows pinched in confusion.

"What?" she asked, frustrated.

"Did you not see me earlier, woman? Did you not see the beast wolf or The Taker that leveled the fucking trees? Did you not see the memory of me sitting in the middle of all that ash? I killed that forest when I was barely out of my teens. My powers have grown ten-fold since then, but you're worried about my safety? It makes no sense."

"Because you haven't been in love before. That's how this works, Asher. If you feel about me the way I feel about you, it's love. I don't give a shit if you can turn into a giant wolf, or if you can level a forest. Odine said you're going to die because of me, and then Blaire, my best friend, whom I trust more than anyone, said Odine's visions are never wrong. So no, I'm not really excited about you going off hunting evil on your own. I feel this gut-deep instinct to keep you close so I can protect you somehow, and it's warring with my head, which is telling me to get away from you so I can keep you safe from myself."

"Give me two days. Mila's calling a Bone-Ripper meeting first thing in the morning to bind the pack to her. I won't be alpha of them. And I'll take my brothers hunting with me if it'll make you feel better. I'll get it done. I'm a good hunter. So is Gentry, so is Roman. Two days, and I'll be back here with you, fate changed, and we can start building that future we both see. Just…don't go."

"Asher—"

"Two days," he begged in a whisper, his clear silver eyes pleading as he shook his head. "You haven't fixed The Taker. You haven't left me weaponless yet, so even if this prediction was really happening, we still have time. Please, Ashlyn."

God, he looked beautiful in the bar light. Like a beautiful, bright-eyed demon, and it was hard to be scared for him when he was here and solid, confident in his hunting abilities. He was so tall, and his arms flexed against his sweater. He was the epitome of strength. And this tough-as-nails, tender monster-indisguise was begging her for time, and how could she deny him? She couldn't. What he'd said made sense. There was time. He was leaving the woods of Winter's Edge, Mila was securing the pack under her, and The Taker was altered, but inside of him was still a weapon of mass destruction that she couldn't imagine any wolf being a threat to. They were attacking every part of Odine's vision in an attempt to change everything about Asher's fate, so how could she look him in those gorgeous blazing eyes and tell the man she loved no?

"Take me home, Asher." Disappointment washed over his features in the moment before she specified, "To ten-ten."

Asher rolled his eyes closed and let off a relieved breath, then leapt over the bar startlingly fast and crushed her to his chest. The jukebox in the corner was playing a soft, slow song, and on the chorus, he gentled his hug and started swaying slightly with her, cupped the back of her hair, and left his lips pressed on the top of her head.

They didn't utter a word for the rest of the song. They didn't have to. This moment with him was settling all her fears that had built up throughout the day, of hearing how uncertain and dangerous his life really was. How hard it was for the Strikers, Blaire, and Mila. For whatever reason, things didn't seem so dark and hopeless when he was here, touching her, reassuring her that everything would be okay. Safe, safe, safe.

"I believe in you," she whispered.

She felt it just as much heard it—the soft, shocked laugh that eased from his chest. "You're the first person who has ever said that."

"To your face."

"What do you mean?"

"Today, Roman and Gentry were listening to Blaire tell me all she knew about you. She was talking about how you kept great power in check. How her inner wolf didn't like getting too close to you because her instincts sometimes said you were scary or off or…"

"Or what?"

"Wrong. But Gentry spoke up immediately, and said you weren't wrong. That you'd never been off. That when you were growing up, even if you hated Gentry, you didn't let anyone fuck with him. You protected him and tried not to let him find out. He told me about these kids bullying him in school freshmen year, and he walked in on you pummeling the shit out of them in the bathroom. He said he knew you didn't mean for him to find out because you looked startled, and you walked out really fast, knocking him in the shoulder as you left. You said, 'What are you looking at, Favorite?' But Gentry said he knew deep down you would have his back if he asked for help. He believes in you."

Asher swallowed audibly and massaged the back of her head as he danced with her to the next slow song that had come on. "And Roman?" he asked. She didn't miss the hope there.

Ashlyn already wanted to cry just thinking of what Roman had admitted. He and Gentry had defended Asher as if they wanted Ashlyn to know how good he was. Or how good he could be. "Roman said when you two got kicked out of the pack, the only thing that kept him going…was you. You gave him an out. You let him escape Rangeley, but he didn't have to do it alone. He told me about that first year when you two were just kids, teenagers, making it on your own. He said he had trouble finding steady work because he was underage, but you worked three jobs so he could finish up his last year of high school in this town on the coast. He said you were working yourself to the bone to pay for a one-bedroom apartment and keep enough food on the table because Roman was on a growth spurt and eating everything to keep his wolf steady. He said you were going through the same, but you would eat less to make sure Roman had enough. When your dad failed, and kicked you out of the pack, you stepped in for Roman, and he knows it. He appreciates it. Roman said he wouldn't be here if it weren't for you propping him up when you two were going through hell in those few years that followed being banished. He told me, 'Asher's always been rogue, but when our lives went to shit, he made me his pack.' So, you see Asher…it's not just me. Your brothers believe in you, too. The people who matter see the good in you."

The song ended on a long note. The jukebox didn't turn over another record, but Asher didn't stop the slow dance. Not for minutes. He just held her in the silence, behind the bar of Winter's Edge. This was one of those moments that changed a life. She'd never noticed one before as it was happening, but deep inside of her, Ashlyn knew this was the exact moment her life took a hard right and went on a different path. One with the potential for destruction, sure, just like every fork in the road had. But it also had the potential for great happiness she could've never imagined before stepping foot in this town blanketed with the supernatural. She'd discovered a world few knew existed, and sometimes it still felt like a dreamscape. Like it was surreal, and she would wake up and wish she was back asleep and dreaming again. But Asher was real, and solid under her arms, his heartbeat thumping against her cheek, his lips soft in her hair, his breath warm against her, his scent crisp and clean. He was the dream she didn't know she'd wanted. Didn't know existed. Didn't know she could have. Didn't know she could wish for.

He was flawed and dangerous and quiet, but gentle with her. He showed her a side of himself he hid from the world, and she'd grown addicted to him. His flaws were now beautiful. And if he was dangerous to others, it was only if they were a threat. She knew—*knew*—he would never hurt her. He was in a fit of rage earlier at Odine, and still, the lethal part of him, The Taker, had left her alone and let her protect Odine, had absorbed some of her goodness at a cost to itself.

"I love you," she whispered, too scared to look in his face.

"Which parts?"

With a private smile, she told him, "I love the wolf. I love The Taker. I love Asher."

"Truth," he murmured. "And now I wish you could see in my head."

"So you wouldn't have to say it out loud, ya chicken?" she joked.

He chuckled and eased back, then brushed a knuckle gently down her cheek. "No, so you could know I'm telling the truth when I say I love everything about you."

"Even my bright clothes?"

He nodded. "Even those."

"Even my sparkly phone case, and my love of make-up? Oh, and my glittery head-bands, my shoe collection, and my frilly coffees?"

"I didn't at first."

"And now?"

"Now I love them. They're you. And you make me happy." He kissed the tip of her nose. "Pretty." He kissed her cheek. "Mate." He lowered his lips to hers and gave her the softest kiss. And when he eased out of it with a faint smack, he tipped his chin toward the door and murmured, "Come on, Sparkles. I want one more good night with you before I start hunting in the morning."

"Oh, you have plans for us tonight then?"

Asher took her hand and led her around the bar top and toward the door. "Yep. Big date plans. I'm about to woo the shit out of you."

She giggled and shook her head as her cheeks heated with pleasure. That man. What he did to the butterflies in her stomach.

Two days, and the uncertainty would be through, but for tonight, she was going to focus on Asher and the time they had together before he left in the morning. Before the bone-deep worry would set in. Before she would pace 1010 for two days obsessing over his safety.

Tonight, it was just her and Asher. Her man, her protector, her love, her beating heart...her mate.

FOURTEEN

"Can I come up there yet?" Ashlyn called up the stairs of 1010. Asher had made her wait down here for ten minutes already.

"No! Wait...yes. Yes, come on up. I'm ready."

"Asher, I swear to God," she muttered, stomping up the stairs, "if you're lying on the bed in some zebra print G-string, I'm out."

But when she made her way into the bedroom, she locked her legs and gaped at the flower petals on the bed, on the floor, and in a trail leading into the bathroom. Candles flickered a soft glow from the dresser, and Asher stood on the other side of the room with his head canted in a very wolf-like manner, eyes silver and locked on her lips, which were gaping open. This looked eerily similar to a fantasy she'd told her bestie Blaire about over cocktails one night.

Suspiciously, she narrowed her eyes as she made her way into the bathroom. The flower petals led to the clawfoot bathtub, and beside it sat a basket with bubble bath and scented bath salts.

She'd definitely been betrayed by her best friend.

"Blaire wasn't supposed to tell anyone about my dream date," she murmured as she turned to find Asher leaning on the open doorframe.

"Why not?"

"Because it was a fantasy, and it was told to her in confidence. We pinky swore not to ever share those."

"But you told me about the cabana boy fantasy."

"That part was a joke. The rest of this..." Ashlyn waved her hand around the room. "That was real. She shouldn't have broken a pinky promise."

"Blaire didn't betray you."

"Well, she's the only one I ever told so—"

Asher leaned down and kissed her forehead. Oooh. Now she got it. "You took it from my mind. Dammit, Asher, you have to stop doing that. Stay out of there. My thoughts are for me."

"I didn't take all of them."

She crossed her arms over her chest and glared. "What do you mean, and why don't you sound sorry?"

"Look. I listened, too." He pulled a bowl of plump, purple grapes from behind his back.

"Gasp! Are you gonna play naughty cabana boy?"

"Told you I was gonna woo the shit out of you."

To the rapid cadence of her pounding heart, she whispered, "I like you."

"Mmmm, now say what you really mean, Sparkles."

"Not until you give me two orgasms."

Asher snorted, and yep, he was definitely blushing as he ducked his gaze to the floor. "You're negotiating?"

Ashlyn arched her eyebrow primly and waited.

"Fine."

"Yes!" she hissed, pumping her fist as she blasted past him. Ashlyn flung herself onto the bed, twisting in mid-air so she could land on her back like a star, and then she said dramatically, "Ravish me. Twice."

"I'm pretty sure you're not supposed to joke this much during sex."

Ashlyn lifted onto her elbows. "I'm pretty sure

you've been doing it wrong then. I spy with my googly eye…" She pointed to his erection pressing against the seam of his jeans.

"You do have ridiculously big eyes."

"Stop. You're only allowed to say nice things to me right now. I'm opening up my treasure palace for you. I spy with my googly eye a boney-macaroni."

"Ashlyn," he admonished, trying to control his smile. "Don't ever, ever call it a macaroni again." Asher made his way to the bed and hovered over her. "You're not turning me on right now."

Ashlyn pointed her finger a few times at his crotch. "Mac says differently."

"Don't."

"He's been named, and now—"

Asher kissed her hard, and oh, she knew exactly what he was doing. He was shutting her up, and a naughty part of her wanted to bite his bottom lip so she could ease back and finish her jokes, but the bigger part of her—the part that found Asher so damn sexy—just wanted to get lost in his touch right now. The teasing was covering up how truly scared she was for him. He probably knew it, and she was glad he hadn't called her out. She wanted to keep her fear quiet and just for herself because fear could make a man weak, and Asher had work to do.

Ashlyn angled her head and parted her lips for him, allowed him to slip his tongue inside as she slid her hands over his shoulders and locked them behind his neck. And then she dragged him closer, so his body weight pressed against hers, and she rocked her hips. A soft, growly groan rattled Asher's chest. Sexy monster.

With one hand, he reached behind himself and pulled his sweater over his head and tossed it to the floor. Without hesitation, and in the same graceful motion, he pushed her sweater up her ribs and plucked it from her head. And then he was instantly on her again as her shirt joined his on the floor.

His powerful legs straddled her hips, but she didn't feel trapped. She felt safe here all surrounded by his strong body. His lips moved against hers like they'd done this a million times, and he had learned exactly what she wanted. God, she loved him. He smiled against her lips, then pressed his tongue inside again and eased himself between her thighs. He made quick work of her jeans, didn't even bother unzipping them, just ripped those mother fuckers down her legs and tossed them. And when he leaned back and gave her a wicked smile, she couldn't help but laugh. She didn't even care what his devilish plans were. She just loved his smile.

Asher trailed nipping, sucking kisses across her jawline to her throat, then to her bra. Asher unsnapped it in the back and yanked that off too. Ashlyn came this close to sighing in relief when her full breasts were freed, but Asher put his mouth on her nipple and sucked gently, and that sigh came out a moan instead. She ran her fingers through his hair and grasped the back of his neck to encourage him. Arching her back against the mattress, she closed her eyes and got lost in the sensation of Asher's lips on her sensitive skin. How had she lived her entire life without this feeling right here? It wasn't just sex. It was making love with The One.

"The one," Asher murmured. When he looked up, he was still smiling, but it had lost the edge of wickedness. It had softened. Sure, he would still terrify small children with those churning silver eyes, but to her, with the candlelight flickering across his face, those beautiful gentle-monster eyes and that breathtaking smile, he was the most beautiful thing she'd ever seen. Beautiful monster.

"Yours," he murmured, kissing down her ribs to her stomach.

"Mmmm," she moaned. She liked that. "Mine."

Asher clamped his mouth over her pink lacy panties, right between her thighs. It was just a moment, and then he eased his mouth off her, but it was enough that her body rolled toward him, begging. "Mine," he growled in an inhuman voice.

He bit down on the waist of her panties and slid them downward. Ashlyn moved her legs as he needed to make the panties slide off smoothly. He trailed tendrils of fire down her skin, following the lace fabric with his fingertips, and the entire time, he held her trapped in that striking gaze of his. It was the sexiest thing she'd ever watched a man do. Oh, he was wooing the shit out of her all right. More like seducing her completely—body, mind, and soul.

His pants went next, and she couldn't help but be struck by the strength of his body. He was big, with defined muscles on his stomach and chest, flexing as he pushed his pants down. He had a defined V-shape right at his hips, and the soft candlelight cast his body in deep shadows and appealing highlights. His massive triceps and shoulders flexed as he settled between her thighs. She'd always been attracted to clean-shaven businessmen with bad attitudes. Men who would never settle because that's what she had wanted, too. No settling, no being tied down to one person. She'd only wanted the aloof types…until Asher.

Now, all she wanted in the world was him and the future they'd talked about.

"Shhhh," he said softly, crawling up her body and pressing his lips to hers. His fingertips were gentle in her hair as he pushed it away from her face. "We'll have it. I'll make sure of it."

She wanted to cry and laugh and hug him tighter. His promise meant so much. Asher thought himself evil, and perhaps he was capable of it, but he cared for her heart more than any man had ever bothered to.

Asher gripped the back of her neck and rolled his hips, slid into her deeply. Ashlyn gasped against his lips at how good he felt inside of her. He pulled out and then pushed back in, over and over until she was writhing and groaning with each thrust. Her orgasm exploded through her, clenching around his thick shaft in fast pulses, and Asher slowed. He drew it out. His teeth were gritted like it was a monumental effort to force himself at the slower pace for her, and she adored him for it. God, he was so sexy, teetering on the edge of his control, taking care of her needs first and pushing his to the side. He loved her back. She could tell.

Something shifted in him, and Asher's control slipped. Perhaps he'd read her mind as she'd determined he was in this with her, too. He slammed into her, and the gentle-monster was gone. Good. She'd gotten the gentle love-making, and now she wanted her man to take his pleasure how he wanted. And apparently, that was hard and fast because he thrust into her deeper and deeper, harder and harder, shoving her up the bed with the force of his movements. He gripped her around the back and crushed her against him as he sucked on her neck hard enough to leave bruises. Her second release came out of nowhere. It just built to blinding within seconds, and she was helpless to do anything but ride the waves of pleasure he created in her body.

She screamed out and dragged her nails down his back how he liked. Asher yelled out and arched his head back as he pushed into her again. Pulsing warmth filled her, throbbing from his dick, heating her from the inside out. She loved this. Loved everything about him. Loved everything about the moments he gave her. Loved how their bodies fit together like they were made for each other. She loved that her Asher was a titan capable of great darkness, but that he was still fighting to remain good. That he was tender with her. That he built her up and kept her steady and cared for her in a way no one else ever had.

He saw her, the real her. And in return, he let her see him, too.

He let her into his darkness, let her be a light, let her expose his shadows and dwell there with him instead of keeping her locked out with the rest of the world.

Minutes passed, and his lips went soft against hers. They sipped at her long after both of their aftershocks had faded away. And then he slid off the bed, lifted her in his arms, and carried her to the bathroom where he drew her a warm bubble bath just like she'd always dreamed of a man doing for her. And as she soaked in the steaming water, he sat beside the tub and watched the curve of her lips, like her smiles fed him, just like his smiles fed happiness to her soul. They didn't say anything, but they didn't have to. She could see his tender thoughts etched into the softness of his darkening eyes. There was no fear or trouble there, which made her feel better about the hunt he would go on. Asher wasn't worried. His head was here, with her.

Ashlyn drew up her knees, crossed her arms over them, and rested her cheek on her forearms so she could drink in his perfect face, his blond, mussed hair, and his beard, only a couple shades darker. His chiseled jaw and muscular neck and tattoos.

"I think you're perfect for me," she whispered.

"Wolf and all?" he asked, the smile slipping a bit.

Ashlyn dipped her chin once.

Asher swallowed audibly and dragged his hand through the water, dislodging a line of bubbles. "I saw your dad."

Ashlyn looked around the room as chills rippled across her arms.

"Not as a ghost. I saw him in your head. It was the night you hung out with Mila and Blaire in Winter's Edge. The night we heard the wolf howl. My instincts were kicked up. I'd felt him before, but then he was too close to you. I wanted to hunt him then, but I couldn't make myself leave you. I watched you through the window. Your worried smile. The way you looked at Mila and Blaire with hurt in your eyes. I didn't feel bad about listening to people's thoughts before you came along, but I saw your dad. More than saw, I felt your pain around the memories. You'd wrapped it up tight with hurt. You talked about me running. You compared me to him. I hated it. I'm not him, Ashlyn."

Ashlyn's eyes burned with tears. Thinking of Dad was unpleasant. "You see too much sometimes, and it scares me."

"Why?"

"Because you're going to see all the bad stuff about me. I can't hide anything from you, Asher. You're going to see it, and you're going to feel differently about me. I want to keep you."

Asher huffed a soft laugh, slid his big, strong hand up her neck, and pulled her close to the edge of the tub. He kissed her gently and then rested his forehead against hers. "Nothing scares me, Ashlyn. The more I get to know you, the more I love you. Tell me about him. Let me in tonight."

"Promise not to run," she whispered. "Promise not to think I'm too much."

"I promise," he said, like it was the easiest oath in the world.

"He was loud and embarrassing when he drank. He moved us out of a nice house to a rat-hole just because he wanted to live closer to his favorite bar. He had friends there, enablers, and he spent a lot of time there. Too much time. I have very few memories of him being sober. My mom was my rock, and I was hers, and in a lot of ways, we still are. We're close because we weathered my father together. I hid him. I never talked about him to my friends at school, never invited anyone over, never had birthday parties like the other kids. I used to pray that my mom would leave him. I saw other kids struggling with their parents divorcing, but I was actually praying for it. I wanted her to move on and find someone who stuck around, who treated her nice, bought her flowers, and didn't always smell like whiskey. One who didn't slur all his words, and who would come home from work every night like a normal husband and eat dinner with us. She didn't leave him until I was in college, though. I was proud of her. I just wished she'd done it sooner. Anyway, he would disappear for weeks at a time. If it went on long enough, we went to the police. He could've been dead under a bridge somewhere for all we knew. It was constant. He missed holidays, just…forgot about them. There was never a time in my childhood where I depended on him to follow through with something and wasn't let down. So when I moved out and went to college, I really *really* wanted a man to make up for all the years of hell he'd put me through. I wanted to believe there was something different than my experience. And I let myself fall in love…God, Asher…this stays between us always, okay? I haven't even told Blaire about this."

"All of your secrets are safe with me, Ashlyn. Tell me about him."

"His name was Jason, and he seemed like a nice boy. At first. I think I was so desperate for a man to be caring and love me that I ignored a lot of red flags. A lot of them. I was determined to be perfect for him, so I could feel this acceptance I'd always wanted. Like I was good enough. I changed everything about me until I didn't recognize myself anymore. It took two years of dating, and I'd snuffed myself out of existence, molded myself into this unfamiliar shape just to fit him. He started cheating, but still I clung to him because I wanted to be good enough, but it hurt worse and worse every time he found a new girl. It took three of them before I ended it, and I thought my life was over. Love was supposed to be this beautiful thing, like in the movies, but for me, it had poisoned me and made me unrecognizable, and for a while I couldn't figure out how to get myself back. The good parts that I'd liked about myself had all been thrown away to make a man happy. So when I finally got them back, I vowed to not get close to a man like that ever again, because love wasn't happiness. It was pain." She shrugged. "Until you, everyone else was faceless."

Asher eased his forehead off hers and slid his bearded jaw against her soft cheek in an animal-like affection. When he settled his lips by her ear, he said, "I'll make you promises. I've never broken one, so you can trust me to follow through. One, I won't ever ask you to change a single thing about yourself because I adore you the way you are. To me, you're perfect. Two, I won't run. What I'm doing tomorrow? That's not running. It's fixing things so I can come back to you and spend the rest of my time trying to make you happy. And three...this is a big one, Sparkles. There won't be anyone but you. Wolves don't work like that. We pick, and that's that. I'll never see anyone else. From here until our last breaths, everyone will be faceless but you. Now...you made a deal, and I followed through with my part. Two orgasms. Your turn. I like to hear the words from your lips. I never got them from other people, and I understand that need for acceptance more than you know. Every time you tell me those three words, the darkness doesn't feel so deep."

Ashlyn smiled and pressed her lips against the scruff on his jaw, stalling until she knew her emotions were steady and her voice wouldn't shake. "Asher Striker, I love you."

He let off a long sigh as if her words were a balm to an ache she hadn't realized he carried. And in a soft, gruff voice, he murmured, "I love you, too."

FIFTEEN

"It's not just one wolf," Gentry murmured from where he knelt in the snow and stared at a set of massive paw prints in the early dawn light. "It's two, maybe three, and none of them smell like Bone-Rippers. Who did you piss off, Asher?"

Who hadn't he pissed off? He'd told Ashlyn he was a PI of sorts, but that wasn't the entire truth. He tracked down bad guys for bad guys. And yeah, some of them were werewolves, so maybe his career choice was coming back to bite him in the ass now.

A nearly translucent Ghost Dad was standing fifteen yards away next to a cover of low brush. He was standing with his profile to them, staring down at the brambles with an empty gaze. Weird. Usually he was staring at him, or at one of his brothers. Ghost Dad liked to be creepy like that.

Asher stood and strode through the fresh snow to where the ghost was standing. A tuft of dark gray fur waved slightly in the breeze. Canting his head, Asher knelt and picked it from the dry thorns, then sniffed.

"Recognize it?" Gentry asked from behind him.

Asher tried to recall his scent again and growled in frustration. It was right at the edge of his tongue, just this faint familiarity. "No," he gritted out.

Roman had knelt quietly beside him, his blazing gold eyes locked on the tuft of fur in Asher's grasp. "Asher didn't piss these wolves off."

"Who did?" Gentry asked.

"No one. They aren't right. They aren't hunting Asher out of vengeance. They're hunting him because they must."

"Who are they?" Asher asked, but from the haunted look in Roman's eyes, he already knew the answer.

"These wolves are from the arena. Slade will be leading them."

"Ssshit," Gentry hissed, pacing away. "Why?" he asked, walking back. "Why do they have to hunt

Asher?"

"Because they've been broken, and now their wolves have to kill other dominants. Any threats have to go."

"I'm not a threat to them."

"You're the biggest of all the wolves, Asher," Roman murmured. "A challenge for broken animals. If they've banded together…" Roman shook his head. "I should've put them down instead of releasing them."

"This isn't your fault," Gentry said low. "You putting them down would've made you go completely dark, and Mila wouldn't have been able to bring you back. How many were there, and what do you know about them?"

"Six males, one female. Female's name is Brayah. She's the least dominant, the weakest link, but a complete brawler, you understand?"

Asher and Gentry looked at each other quick, then nodded. Roman was saying there was a pack of bloodthirsty war dogs about to rain down on them. "They'll work more like a wild pack because the human in them was ripped out by the way they were pitted against each other. Unnecessary fighting drags the wolf to the surface, and the good parts go away. They aren't recoverable. You don't fight like that, kill for sport like that, and then go back to a normal life. You stay empty." Roman's roiling gold eyes had gone vacant as he stared off into the trees.

"You didn't stay empty," Asher pointed out quietly.

"I was in there only a couple days, and I came out of it to Mila, who wouldn't quit on bringing me back. I was the new fighter. The others were fucked beyond repair before I even went in there. Especially the two titans Anderson had built up."

"Titans?"

"They're rippers. Anderson started them easy on submissive wolves. Built up their tolerance to killing and pitted them against more and more wolves as they gained their confidence and lost their humanity. They were his prize fighters. His Beasts, he called them. Slade and Carver. Anderson called him Bone-Carver in the arena, but it'll probably be Slade leading the pack. He was an alpha before he was captured. Gentry, if you're only seeing two, maybe three wolves, my guess is the others didn't just split off. Slade and Carver would've killed them. They may *have* to kill now just to sate the wolves."

"Dammit, Roman," Gentry gritted out. "Why didn't you tell us then? Asher and I could've put them down instead of letting them being unleashed onto the world."

"It wasn't their fault, Gentry! They didn't put themselves in those cages or fight willingly. Not until their minds had been taken completely. You weren't there, sitting in that damn cell, drowning in the fucking stink of fear and piss. We were all scared but the Beasts, and you can bet your ass when they were in the beginning stages of being turned monster, they were scared, too. I guess I really wanted…"

"Wanted what, Roman," Asher asked. "Just say it."

"I wanted maybe one of them to be okay, and who was I to choose who had a shot at that? I was just the lucky asshole who got sold to Anderson last."

"All right, Asher, how do you want to play this?" Gentry asked, linking his hands behind his head.

Asher frowned in suspicion. "Roman said they'll be like a pack of wild wolves. Right up your ally, Wolf Hunter. I thought you would want to take lead on this one."

"First off, thanks for calling me Wolf Hunter and

not Favorite, because I hate that fucking nickname, and second, you're basically alpha wolf here. Even if I came up with a plan of attack, you could make us do whatever you want anyway, so what's the point? Plus…" Gentry shrugged and left the rest unspoken.

Asher had to know, though. "Plus what?"

Gentry ran his hands over his hair and flung them off his head in discomfort. "You know…"

Asher arched his eyebrows, and Roman muttered something about, "emotional constipation and therapy hour," as he dug deeper into the brambles.

"Just say it," Asher demanded. "And I swear to God if you're about to call me evil, or Asherhole, I'm gonna bust you in the face."

"Man, forget it," Gentry muttered, doing an about face. "Fuck you, Asherhole."

"Tell me!"

"I was going to say I trusted you," Gentry barked out as he rounded on him. "I fucking trust you, man. You're the one being hunted, you're as good a hunter as me and Roman, maybe better because, yeah, you're probably fuckin' evil."

"At least a little evil," Roman agreed.

Okay, the evil comment made his wolf want to rip

both their throats out, but Gentry had just said he trusted him, and he'd never said anything like that before. Not to Asher's face. It drew him up straight and left him speechless.

Roman stood and started shadow boxing Ghost Dad, who stood there staring at the bushes, looking bored.

"Leave the ghost alone," Asher said.

"Or what?" Roman asked. "I'm boxing with my old man. It's quality father-son time, like when we were kids. Oh wait, we didn't get that because he was an ass-face."

"To protect Asher," Gentry said. He frowned when Roman kicked Dad in the ghost dick. "What's wrong with you?"

"What's wrong with me? We're standing around having brother time instead of hunting the mother fuckers who are hunting us."

"Asher," Gentry gently reminded him. "They're hunting Asher."

"Psychodine saw it. We'll be bloody in the snow next to his corpse. Mila's going to miss you," Roman said to Asher through a grin. His voice dripped with sarcasm when he said, "She likes your sense of humor."

"Fuck you," Asher muttered.

"Maybe we'll dump your ashes in the woods like you did to Dad," Roman called as Asher made his way back down the trail they'd walked. "What do you want to eat for your last meal? Say 'pussy.' It'll be funny."

Gentry snorted behind him, but Asher ignored them both and barely resisted the urge to snap his fingers and draw in all the ghosts within a one mile radius to rush Roman and scare the shit out of him. Asher did have a sense of humor—it was just an *evil* one.

"Where are we going?" Gentry called.

"You asked me what our play was."

"And?"

"We need to find their den and flush those mother fuckers out."

"And then what?" Gentry asked.

Asher clenched his fists and ducked a low-hanging branch. He had two days until he'd promised Ashlyn this would be over. He'd never broken an oath, and he'd be damned if he started with his mate. "And then we go to war."

SIXTEEN

"Okay, if the Bone-Rippers hate humans, can you two explain to me again why I have to be at this meeting?" Ashlyn asked in an octave above what she'd intended. "And why on God's green and blue planet would any organization call themselves the Bone-Rippers? That's terrifying."

"Rhett, the last alpha, came up with the name," Mila explained from where she was setting a massive plate of grilled cheeses on the bar top of Winter's Edge.

"And what happened to him again?"

"I killed him," Mila said with a flat smile.

The sweet, soft-spoken, submissive little brunette turned and bustled back into the kitchen, leaving

Ashlyn to stare after her. "Oh. She killed him."

Blaire was staring at her with a crease of worry between her eyebrows. "I know this is a lot, Ashlyn, but you're a part of this now. Mila is nervous, and she's about to try and bring a broken wolf pack under her. She's submissive, and it's a scary thing for her to do. This isn't something she ever planned or wanted."

"Not at all," Mila murmured as she returned from the kitchen with two giant serving trays of crinkle cut french fries. "I would rather cut off both my pinky toes than do what I'm about to do, but if it protects Asher..." She inhaled deeply, lifting her chest and shoulders with it, then exhaled. "Then I'll do this alpha gig. And you're here because A, we are under strict orders from the Dark Wolf to not let you out of our sight, and he scares me, and B, if I'm gonna be alpha, I'm doing things way different than Rhett did. And that includes being closer to humans. He separated us and made it hard for us to fit in with the human world. That shit's a-changin' today."

"And you're using me to change said shit?" Ashlyn guessed.

Mila handed her a warm grilled cheese sandwich and smiled brightly. "Yep. You're with Asher. No point in hiding it, right? The boys' father hid his marriage to Odine for a long time, and he was really careful, but they still got caught. I figure if you two just come out now as a couple, people will be shocked at first, but settle eventually, especially if I'm alpha and can order them to get the fuck over it. I think it's about time someone re-wrote the rules."

Hmm. Ashlyn liked Mila even more now.

The door of Winter's Edge swung open, and in walked seven men and women of varying heights and ages, led by an older gentleman with bushy gray eyebrows and green eyes that were sharp and seemed to miss nothing as he scanned the bar.

"I *am* the big bad wolf," Mila whispered to herself as she watched the others approach.

The Bone-Rippers were looking around the bar, murmuring low amongst themselves, moving too damn gracefully. Ashlyn would look like a bumbling rhino next to any of them. Some of them had strange eye colors and one, a man about her age, had his lip snarled up. He was probably growling, but she couldn't hear him from where she stood behind the bar with Blaire and Mila. She was getting more than a few dirty looks, though, so she held up a pad of paper and whispered to Blaire, "I'm just going to be over here, coming up with better pack names."

"She knows?" the older gentleman asked, fury transforming his features until his face was twisted up like a predator.

"Eeee," Ashlyn muttered, sidestepping back toward Blaire again. "If they attack me, bite the shit out of them okay?"

Blaire snorted and said, "I've got you."

Now, Ashlyn was a stress-eater, and had been ever since she was a kid, so she shoved a good third of that grilled cheese into her mouth and began rapidly chewing. She probably looked like a squirrel right now, but hang it. The Bone-Rippers were scary as hell.

"What's this meeting about?" the older man said. He must've been some kind of leader because the others had grown silent and watchful as they'd lined up behind the bar top on the other side.

"I killed Rhett," Mila said in a surprisingly strong voice. "He's gone because of me, and I'm claiming the throne."

The man arched one bushy brow up high. "Mmm, no."

"What? Tim, alpha is mine by right. I want to do the binding ceremony today. Right now."

"But you took too long to claim it, Mila. Someone else got to your throne first. The crown isn't up for grabs anymore."

"Who claimed it? You?"

Tim shook his head slowly, and now some of the others smiled, but not friendly expressions. It was more a show of teeth. Sharp teeth. There was so much tension in the room it was hard to breathe, and no one was speaking.

They were all having some staring contest Ashlyn didn't understand, so to break the silence, she laughed nervously and announced, "I've come up with some new pack name ideas." Everyone turned to look at her. "I mean, let's face it. Bone-Rippers isn't a good name from a PR standpoint. I was thinking…" She read the names she'd come up with on the fly off the notepad. "Glitter dogs?" Nobody moved, and nobody spoke. "Right." She marked that one off with a flourish of her pen. "Love Nuggets, Sexy Unicorns, or oh! Here's my favorite…The Pupcakes. Get it? It's like cupcakes…but…" The air was filled with the snarling of werewolves, so she pursed her lips and silenced herself. At least Blaire snorted a tiny giggle. She cut off the sound almost immediately, but it counted.

"If you aren't alpha, then who is?" Mila gritted out to Tim.

A lady with fluffed-up gray hair gave a shrill whistle that made Blaire and Mila hunch their shoulders and cover their ears. The door to Winter's edge flung open and crashed against the wall, and the biggest man she'd ever laid eyes on ducked under the doorframe. He was roughly the size of a house, pushing seven-foot tall. He had tattoos down both arms and up his neck, and his black hair was fashioned into a laid-down mohawk.

"Slade," Mila said in a frightened tone that made Ashlyn look at her in confusion. Mila's face had gone white as a sheet, and she was backing up step after slow step, her eyes wide and locked on the giant.

Behind the man trailed another giant, and another, and then a tall, lanky woman who walked hunched over, attention twitching this way and that, her eyes blazing an inhuman shade of fiery gold. All their faces were twisted into something fearsome, like they were midway through a Change into their wolves already. And now Ashlyn really couldn't breathe.

"Slade is our alpha now, Mila," Tim said in a snarl.

Slade's predatory eyes were locked on Ashlyn, and all she wanted to do was duck behind the counter and wish this all away. He was that terrifying. She couldn't move, couldn't breathe.

"You're the other alpha's bitch," the man said in a deep, rumbling voice.

Ashlyn shook her head and stammered. "A-alpha?"

The man was still stalking forward, coming closer. *Move, feet!* He cocked his head and narrowed his eyes to thin slits. "Asher Striker, alpha of the Wolves of Winter's Edge. This is my town now. I want his territory, I want his pack, and you'll get them for me."

Blaire slipped her hand around Ashlyn's and raised her voice. "Asher's not alpha. He's rogue. We all are."

"Bullshit. I was there the night you came to the arena, White Wolf. I felt the bond. Practically saw it. Asher's a right proper monster. He has powers, right? I saw him do things no man or wolf should be able to do." He turned his dead gaze on Ashlyn. "Nah, human bitch. He's alpha, and you're his mate. We've done our research. Your job is simple. Easy. Painless. I just need you to bring him to me."

Painless? Betraying Asher would rip her heart out. "Fuck you."

"Maybe after your mate's dead." Slade tipped his head to the side and dragged a hungry gaze to her chest, then back to her eyes. "I don't usually like leftovers, but I already know you can bed a monster. And I have a big"—he inhaled, his nostrils flaring slightly with the breath as he seemed to search for the right word—"appetite."

"Ashlyn, run." Blaire had said it so softly Ashlyn thought she'd imagined it. Right up until Blaire turned to her and squeezed her hand so hard Ashlyn yelped. Blaire's eyes were blazing such a vivid green they were hard to look at. Louder, she demanded, "Run now." She shoved her toward the kitchen door, and before Ashlyn could even get her legs moving, Blaire fell to the floor with a snarl in her chest, and the massive snow-white wolf ripped from her body. Already Mila was Changed into a mottled gray wolf and leaping through the air at Slade. Shit, shit, shit.

Ashlyn hit the door hard and sprinted through

the kitchen, but she could hear someone following right behind her. Could feel their closeness. Could almost feel their breath on her neck. She whimpered and skidded around one of the stainless-steel counters as she struggled the big skull pocket knife Asher had given her out of her pocket. The gold-eyed woman was right on her, but she slid farther than her and gave Ashlyn those precious seconds to shove the back door open.

Her mind racing a million miles a minute, Ashlyn flipped the blade out. She didn't have much time, because the woman was so fast. Could Asher read her mind from this far? Where was he? *Don't come back here.*

Everything was settling into place. Asher was alpha? It wasn't alpha of the Bone-Rippers like they'd thought. He was unknowingly alpha of the damn Wolves of Winter's Edge. And these empty-eyed werewolves were going to use her to draw him back here, where he was supposed to die. No, no, no.

She pushed her legs as hard as she could, but her boots were sinking deep into the un-marred snow.

"Asher, don't come back here!" she screamed as the woman grabbed her hair and yanked her backward.

The second Ashlyn was spun around, she slammed the blade into her shoulder. The woman howled in pain, and her eyes flashed with fury in the second before her fist smashed into Ashlyn's face. The shock of the pain brought her to her knees in the snow.

So dizzy. She didn't want to open her eyes, but the woman was dragging her now by the hair, and all Ashlyn could do was hold onto her wrists to give her scalp some relief. Red was dripping onto her pink sweater. Red polka dots from her bleeding nose. It must've been broken, it hurt so badly. The woods around her were spinning slowly. "Don't come back here," she pleaded in a whisper, concentrating on the thought as hard as she could.

"Brayah, do you have her?" a voice called.

"Got her," the woman snarled, yanking a struggling Ashlyn up to her feet and bullying her to move faster.

Around the corner of the building, some of the Bone-Rippers had gathered outside. A couple of gray wolves slunk along the edge of the tree line, and from a trail that led to the inn strode two more men.

"Are they at the inn?" Slade asked.

One of the men shook his head. "The place is totally empty."

"Fuck!" Slade looked like shit. His shoulder was bleeding badly, and there were claw marks all over his face and neck. She would've been proud of Blaire and Mila, but they weren't out here, and all she felt right now was worry over their safety. As it stood, there was an enormous racket inside, glass breaking, furniture hitting the walls, but Mila and Blaire weren't where Ashlyn could see them. All she could hope was they were still inside fighting, not lying stiff in a corner while the Bone-Rippers trashed Winter's Edge.

Don't come for me.

"What do you want to do?" Brayah asked, jerking Ashlyn to a stop near Slade, digging an unforgiving grip deep into Ashlyn's neck, like she wanted to snap it. She probably could with little effort. "If he has too much warning, Asher could disappear on us."

"Nah, not without his mate," Tim said from where he was nursing a gaping cut across his cheekbone. "The Strikers bond hard. As long as you have his human, he'll come."

"Good," Slade said, flinging blood off his fingertips into the snow. Red on white. Ashlyn wanted to retch. "Then we'll take her out into the woods and make her scream. Brayah," Slade said, gesturing to her like ladies first. "Lead the way."

"With pleasure, Alpha," Brayah said in a dead voice that matched her vacant eyes. Something was seriously wrong with her.

The Bone-Rippers were Changing. More and more wolves trotted alongside of them through the trees. Gray ones and dark brown ones, and one was even black. Not demon-black like Asher's monster wolf, but a patchy black with chocolate brown points and a gray muzzle.

Don't come back.

A whimper crawled up her throat as Brayah gripped the back of her neck and forced her to move forward faster. Her nails dug into Ashlyn's skin and made her hunch her shoulders against the stinging pain. She had to get out of this, had to escape somehow. Desperately, she looked around for something, anything to use as a weapon, but even if she could bend down to pick one up with Brayah's hand gripping her neck, there were now seven wolves surrounding her and closing in, eyes intent on her, hungry, as they snapped their razor-sharp teeth and snarled at her.

Pack of monsters. The Strikers were the good ones. They would never look at a human like this. They would never hunt and hurt one. These wolves were bad. They wanted to hurt her, to kill her, to bleed her. She could tell by the rising excitement in their eyes and the pitch of their yipping. Two began to howl, as though she was their prey.

Don't come back. Please, Asher, don't come back to Winter's Edge.

Two of the gray-colored wolves broke out in a fight near her, brawling and ripping each other to shreds. The sound of the growling and the violence scared her, and her emotions suddenly overwhelmed her. She huffed a fear-filled breath that froze in front of her face. It was so cold out here, even the tears that streamed down her cheeks were only warm for a moment before they froze. Her jacket was back in Winter's edge, and now she couldn't stop shivering from both the cold and adrenaline.

They were going to hurt her. She knew it with certainty. Was this the place she was going to meet her end? With these strangers in the cold, haunted woods of Rangeley? Torn to little pieces by creatures she hadn't even known existed until a few days ago?

And all for what? So they could hurt the man she loved? So they could get to her mate?

She hated them. Hated their emptiness, hated their hatred. If she had The Taker in her, she would devour every last one of them right now and not feel an ounce of guilt.

Up in the sky, the clouds began to darken by the moment, roiling slowly like they were forming a twister. And she could feel him. It was as if her soul recognized its counterpart was near.

Asher was here.

The Taker was here.

Odine had been right.

A long, low howl lifted the fine hairs on her body. The reaction of the wolves around her was instant. The snarling stopped, and all their attention went to the east in the direction of the battle cry. A second howl joined the first, rising in haunting notes and then lowering back down again. Two wolves. Just two. Maybe it was just Gentry and Roman, and they'd left Asher somewhere safe. That was just wishful thinking, though. It wasn't logic. The clouds were dark and menacing, and it looked like evening instead of ten in the morning.

"He's here," Slade said from behind them as Brayah jerked Ashlyn to a stop. Her neck trickled warmth where the woman's nails dug in, but she couldn't worry about that right now.

The prophesy was coming true. From the day of his birth, Asher had been building to this moment. To the moment of his death.

A storm wall formed in the east. Snow and dark blue fog blotted out the landscape, but two figures appeared out of the chaos. A charcoal gray wolf with bright green eyes and a light gray wolf with a golden gaze trotted toward them, heads down, hatred in their eyes. And behind them followed Asher, human, hands out, dressed in dark jeans and the black sweater. His arms bulged with tension as he lifted his palms, and all around him, the fog whipped like a hurricane wind, reaching from his body and absorbing back into him in a constant chaotic cadence. It stretched as far as she could see, and as he passed, the trees around him splintered, dried, fell, and turned to ashes.

Asher was feeding in preparation to bring hell to the wolves here.

His eyes were a smoldering silver, like mercury in his face. Ashlyn had never seen fury on a man's face like this.

"Kill them," Slade demanded through a smile that made no sense to Ashlyn. Didn't he see the motherfucking storm named Asher coming for him? Didn't he see his death coming? Didn't he care?

The wolves around her took off at a dead sprint toward the wall of power. No...toward Gentry and Roman, who were now charging toward them with the promise of death in their eyes. Seven wolves on two, but the Striker brothers weren't normal werewolves. They were nearly twice the size of the others, with long strides and big, powerful barrel chests.

They clashed in a mess of brutality. The animals spun and ripped and snarled and were hurled from the battle. Some got up and returned, while some stayed broken in the snow.

"Let go of me," Ashlyn screeched, yanking out of Brayah's grasp. Her nails tore her skin, but so what? She couldn't stand here and not help! She bent as fast as she could, but the woman was on her. Ashlyn picked up a heavy branch and swung it upward, caught Brayah in the side of the face. She'd thought it would only buy her a second, but the woman went hurling toward a tree, slammed into the trunk with a horrible crack of bone, then slid down into the snow and didn't get up. Chest heaving, Ashlyn looked down at the stick, but it was covered in dark blue fog. Asher was somehow bolstering her strength, giving her the ability to protect herself. When she looked up, something awful was happening in the woods. Ghosts were gathering by the hundreds, closing in on them, all transparent and dead-eyed.

"What the fuck?" Slade said on a breath as he scanned the haunted forest. "Carver, you can see this too…right?"

The other giant, the one who was almost as big as Slade, nodded his head once. "I see 'em."

"Asher's power is bringing in the dead," Ashlyn said desperately. "Run now and live." *Run now so Asher can live!*

Slade lunged for her, but Ashlyn had seen it coming and lurched out of his way, took off running, tossing her stick at him as she bolted. He was on her fast, though, and his grip was painful around her arm as he yanked her to a stop and slammed her back against a tree so hard her head snapped back and smashed into the rough bark. With a gasp at the pain, Ashlyn shook her head to try to clear her vision.

Slade slid an evil smile to Asher, who was running toward her now. The black wolf exploded from his body in a smattering of popping bones and reshaping flesh. The fog seeping out of him darkened and thickened as he sprinted for them, his eyes white as the snow. Something bad was happening but she couldn't think straight. Hell, she couldn't even see straight. There were two of Slade now. She blinked hard as she struggled against him with all her strength. It was like she'd fallen into the back of a cement truck, cement had dried all over her body, and now she was trying to break free of it.

Don't let him bite you, Ashlyn! Asher's scream was so loud in her head she jumped, but his warning came too late. Slade's face morphed into a horrid gray wolf as he shifted right there against her. And then the flash of white teeth was so fast she had no time to react. His fangs pierced her neck one second before Asher's Dark Wolf barreled into Slade's gray one.

Ashlyn was ripped to the ground with the force of their collision. Carver Changed into a dark brown wolf, a massive one, and leapt onto the frenzied battle Asher was fighting with Slade. Two more wolves bolted out of the woods and joined them, and now it was four on one.

Ashlyn was helpless as she watched her mate fight for his life. For hers. She would've given anything to save him, but her body wasn't working right anymore. Her neck was on fire, as if she'd lit a blow torch and swallowed the flame. Warmth streamed down her neck, and in shock, she lifted her hand to the bite to try to staunch the bleeding. Why did it hurt this bad? Fire crackled down her neck to her chest and settled there for a few moments like dragon's fire as she watched Asher in horror. He was a pitch-colored, rip-roaring, murder machine. He spun and engaged and bit and ripped like he'd been born to end life.

Her legs stopped working, and Ashlyn couldn't get up out of the cold snow. Crimson on white. It would've been kind of beautiful if she wasn't dying. And oh, she was dying. She could feel it. No one could endure pain like this for long and survive.

The soft murmured chanting of a witch filled her senses, and now she could see her—Odine. She was standing near a tree Asher had devoured and felled, her hands out, palms up, eyes rolled back in her head. Snow lifted from the ground and whipped around the chaos in the woods. The navy fog rolled from Asher in a massive wave, and the wolves he fought stopped moving. They just dropped and withered to gray corpses in moments. Blaire and Mila's wolves streaked through the trees and barreled into the fight Gentry and Roman were still waging, and with the flick of her fingers, Odine tossed one of the wolves from the pile. His body pitched high into the air, and a sharp death whine sounded when he pummeled back to earth again.. Gentry was lying motionless in the snow, chest rising raggedly, while Blaire placed her massive, white-furred, snarling body over her mate and glared at the gray wolf stalking him. Roman and Mila were at war with two of the Bone-Rippers, while ghosts converged on the clearing. Ashlyn could barely see through the phantoms now. They surrounded her and blocked out everything, and now she was alone, facing a transparent man with eyes like Asher's. He knelt slowly in front of her as the dark blue fog filled up all the extra space and covered up the ghosts around them. The Taker didn't touch her, though. He didn't touch Asher's father either.

The ghost smiled sadly and parted his lips. "You're going to be okay. My boy will fix you. He was meant to fix you, Ashlyn. His whole life, everything that happened, everything I did, every decision he made, has led him to you. You gave him light. You made my son happy."

"It's not enough time," she sobbed, her hair whipping around her shoulders. "I didn't have him long enough." Over the roaring wind, she yelled, "It's not fair!"

"Some lives aren't fair, Ashlyn. He loves you, though, like I love my Odine. Never forget his gift. Never forget the sacrifice, but always remember, to him, you're worth it." He smiled, and the lines around his blue eyes deepened. "Tell Asher I always loved him. Roman, too. I just didn't want today to come. I fought it, and they paid for my fear by feeling unloved. My boys and their mother were my whole world. Even in my afterlife, they're my world."

The ghost stood slowly and backed away, disappearing into the fog. "Tell him," the ghost's words echoed in her head.

The pain was unbearable now, wrecking every cell in her body. Blaire had described this when she'd told Ashlyn about being bitten. It was so much more excruciating than she could've ever imagined.

Ashlyn pitched forward, but two strong arms caught her right before she hit the snow. Asher was here, looking down at her with panic in his silver eyes. "No, no, no. Ashlyn, stay with me." He looked up into the chaos. "Odine!"

"Why don't you call her Mom?" Ashlyn asked in a whisper. She'd always wondered that.

Asher dragged his gaze back to her. "Because I was angry with her for a long time."

"I'm supposed to tell you something important, Asher."

"No, no, don't say goodbyes, baby. You aren't going anywhere. Odine!"

"Your dad told me to tell you he loves you. He always did. He was just scared of today. He loves you, Asher."

Asher shook his head over and over. When he looked back at her, his eyes were rimmed with moisture, and he looked heartbroken. "I'm going to fix this. I'm going to heal you, okay, Ashlyn? Just like when you cut your hand, but bigger. I'm going to raise your wolf."

"Will it hurt you?" she asked.

Asher gave her the saddest smile and shook his head. "I asked Odine that once, a long time ago, when she was gonna try to fix me. I'll tell you the same thing she told me. It'll hurt how it has to, but I would do anything for you."

"Asher," she whispered.

"This is how it's supposed to be. Shhhh." He cradled her head in his lap and rocked her as she sobbed. "You are light and good, and you're supposed to stay in this world, Ashlyn. It's not done with you yet."

The blue fog swirled faster and began to gather above them in a churning storm cloud. A ghost close to them whispered, "A storm is coming."

And another one answered, "The storm is here."

And then the massive cloud that had once dwelled inside of the man she loved—The Taker— plummeted to earth and blasted through her body. It hurt. Oh, it hurt, and she couldn't draw a breath.

"Shhh, listen to my voice," Asher said in a pained

tone as he held her, rocking gently. "We're running together as wolves. We're living here, in ten-ten. Every Friday night I take you out to dinner, and for coffee after, the kind you like. And every night I wrap you up in my arms and talk to you until you go to sleep. And when the wolf needs out, we Change together. We run together, Ashlyn. I'll always be with you." His voice grew weaker as she felt something other ripping out of her. "I'm not running. I'll be waiting for the world to be done with you."

And then Asher's voice faded to nothing, his touch disappeared, and the thing inside of her escaped.

The woods dipped to silence in the span of a moment. There was no more war, no more chaos. There were no bodies, only ash and a lightened sky. The snow settled over the destroyed landscape, and around them, not a single tree remained upright.

Ashlyn looked down at a body that didn't work right. Her paws were black as pitch. Demon black like the wolf who had sacrificed his life for hers. She huffed a broken sob as she looked at Asher lying in the snow. He wasn't breathing, and she felt no life from him. Her heart shattering completely. She did the only thing this body knew how to do. She sang for him, lifting her howl higher and higher, closing her eyes against the world, because she knew without a shadow of a doubt she would never be okay again. She would never be whole.

The other Wolves of Winter's Edge were broken and bloodied but standing. Blaire tossed her head back and howled with Ashlyn, and one by one, the others joined. It was the saddest song ever sung.

Odine limped to Asher's body and fell onto the snow beside him. Her hair was nearly white, and she was crying. "I waited for so long for him to choose a side of the fence. Good or evil. I could never guess where he would end up, and look what he's done. My good boy wasn't The Taker in the end, was he?" Tears streamed down her cheeks as she cradled his body to her. "He was The Giver." She smiled at Ashlyn, dislodging two more tears. "You did that for him, and for that, I'm going to give you a gift. I'm going to give him a gift, too. I'm going to give you that future you both wanted. I couldn't see it before, but I can see it so clearly now. Promise me you'll always keep him on the good side of the fence, Ashlyn. Keep him steady. You're the only one who can."

Odine offered her a sad smile, then placed her hand on Asher's chest and closed her eyes, then began chanting something under her breath. The other wolves came and stood in a half circle behind Odine, and soft white mist began to pour from them and into Asher. When Ashlyn looked down at her own body, the same was happening with her blue. And from Odine, clouds of thick black poured from her and into her son.

And in the exact moment Asher dragged a ragged breath into his lungs, Odine's body turned to ash and floated gently away in the breeze.

Ashlyn's body collapsed in on itself with blinding pain as her wolf tucked itself away. She didn't know if the Change took moments or hours, but as soon as she was able, she pushed up on her hands and knees and opened her eyes, searching for Asher. He sat just a few yards away, looking pale as the ghosts that had been drawn to his dark magic. He was shaking, but it was his exhausted smile that told her everything was going to be okay.

"Asher," she whispered. She tackled him, sobbing so hard her shoulders shook.

"It's okay. It's over," he murmured, hugging her

tightly against him, petting her hair and rubbing his jaw against her cheek.

It wasn't all okay, though. "Asher, your mom…"

He eased back and cupped her cheeks, searched her eyes, and then twitched his chin toward the woods. "She's okay. She's where she wants to be."

Ashlyn turned on his lap. Odine's ghost stood straight and tall, looking decades younger, her black hair whipping around her shoulders in a strong wind that Ashlyn didn't feel. She was smiling slightly, her dark eyes dancing with joy as she held the hand of Asher's father.

They both looked so happy.

"Great, now we get to be haunted by both of them," Roman said testily from where he stood butt naked with his hands on his hips.

Mila laughed emotionally from beside him where she clutched onto his arm affectionately. "Come on, Roman. It's romantic. They're finally back together again, and look how sweet they are."

Gentry was torn all to hell, bleeding from a dozen places, and was sitting in the snow looking like death warmed over. Blaire was kneeling behind him with her arms around his neck, propping him up, as they watched the ghosts.

"I'm not supposed to be able to see them," Gentry said gruffly.

"Welcome to the club, Favorite," Roman said softly. "Asher probably made us all into demons with that crazy shit he just pulled. Now we're all probably a little bit evil. Thanks for that, Asherhole."

Asher didn't respond. In fact, none of them did. They all dipped into a heavy silence to match the woods around them. No one spoke, or moved to leave. Maybe everyone was too drained, or perhaps they just needed this time to accept what had happened here. In the span of half an hour, everything had changed.

Ashlyn clung to her mate, inhaling his scent and memorizing it with her new heightened senses, while around them, ashes kicked up with every movement of the cold breeze.

At last, Asher said, "Let's go home," and struggled to his feet with Ashlyn's help. He kissed the side of her head, draped an arm over her shoulder, and began to make his way slowly back toward the inn.

When Ashlyn looked behind her, Roman and Mila and Gentry and Blaire were following right behind.

"I'm a werewolf now," Ashlyn muttered in shock. "Today was super-fuckin' weird."

Blaire giggled behind her, and Mila joined in too. Gentry and Roman chuckled softly and just like that, the heavy moment was lightened.

"At least you're a pretty werewolf," Blaire said unhelpfully.

"The prettiest one I've ever seen," Asher said low as he smiled down at her.

Ashlyn snorted. "Cheeseball. You can't say that about a wolf that looks identical to yours."

"Yeah, man, way to be really conceited," Roman offered.

Asher sighed tiredly, but he was still smiling.

"So, when are we going to stop calling ourselves rogues?" Blaire asked. "Because Asher is definitely our alpha."

"Now's good with me," Gentry said.

"Fuck it, we're in," Roman muttered, hugging Mila tight against his side.

And at that moment, the sun decided to peek out from behind the clouds, casting the ash-covered Winter's Edge woods in rays of light. In rays of hope.

"Are you happy?" Asher asked softly. He was

looking down at her lips with the softest expression in his eyes.

"I'm relieved that I get to keep you," she whispered emotionally. She blinked hard to keep her tears to herself, and then twitched her head behind them. "And that I get to keep them, too. Today could've gone so differently." She could've lost everything back there. It had been so damn close.

Asher pulled her close and kissed the top of her head. "Today went exactly how it was supposed to."

"What now?" she asked.

"Now, we get some clothes on."

Ashlyn looked down and huffed a laugh. "Yeah, we're mega-naked right now."

"Nudity is natural," Roman pointed out.

"And then we're going to clean up and eat," Asher said.

"And then sleep," Blaire said helpfully. "I could sleep for three days."

"Okay, selfish," Roman muttered. "Asherhole was the only one here who actually died. I mean, he was flatlined for at least a minute. But Blaire thinks she's the one who needs a nap—"

Ashlyn giggled and turned around in time to see

Blaire blast him in the back of the head with a snowball.

"I'm not selfish. Odine drained us all to save him, Roman," Blaire admonished him.

"Technically," Mila offered, "she probably drained Blaire more than you, Roman. She's the White Wolf, all pure and goodness. Odine could probably only use about half of your tainted mojo."

"Whose side are you on, mate?" he growled, nipping at his mate's ear as she giggled. "You owe me thirty BJs now."

"And then what?" Ashlyn asked Asher quietly as the banter behind them continued.

"And then I'm going to ask you stay here, with me, in ten-ten. And we're going to finally open up Winter's Edge and get this place running again. All of us. Together. And after that, you and I are going to get started living that future we talked about."

She smiled up at her mate, and then she uttered the words of her heart—the ones he'd told her he longed for all the time. The ones that fed his soul and gave her good smiles. "I love you."

Asher eased them to a stop and allowed the others to pass, and then he cupped her neck and kissed her gently. When at last he eased back, he told her, "I'll never run, Ashlyn. I love you more than anything."

And she knew it was true, because he'd used that love to save her life. For a moment, she was overwhelmed because, now, their future stretched on and on. A future she'd never even dreamed she could have. They were both safe, and a part of something bigger, together. They were a part of a pack, part of the inn, and a part of the bar his father had left as a legacy for his sons.

Before they'd met, they had both been rogues in their own way—lonely, both believing they were destined to walk this earth alone, both afraid to trust, or love deeply. But somehow, against all odds, they'd found each other, and then they'd fought for each other.

Today, good had won, evil had lost, and love had prevailed. Their pack had weathered the storm and taken the town back. There were no more broken Bone-Rippers or murderous beasts to taint Rangeley.

Now, there were only the Wolves of Winter's Edge.

EPILOGUE

"Okay, everyone, say cheese," Blaire sang as she pushed the button on the camera that was sitting up on a tripod in the snow.

"If we have our backs to the camera, why would it matter if we smiled?" Roman asked testily.

Ashlyn giggled and rested her head on Asher's shoulder as they sat on the edge of a cliff and looked out over the snowy hills. This picture was for her. This had been a special place for the Strikers, and now for the Wolves of Winter's Edge Pack, but Asher had asked for them to retake the photo so she could be in it. He'd said the other picture, "Doesn't feel finished without you."

So here they sat, on the eve of the opening of

ASHER

Winter's Edge, taking a picture out in the freezing cold. The three pairs—Blaire and Gentry, Roman and Mila, and Asher and her—were sitting all together, shoulders touching as they looked out at the sunset. The sun was just a sliver of light and was painting the sky in the prettiest neon colors.

Right before the click of the camera, Asher put his arm around her and turned, pressed his lips onto the side of her hair. *Click*.

Ashlyn had closed her eyes the moment his lips touched her. He made her feel that good. The last month spent here with him, helping the pack clean up the damage the Bone-Rippers had done to Winter's Edge, had been the happiest of her life. It was days spent getting to know a town she was falling hard for. A town she wanted to build a future in. It was spending time with her pack, feeling like a part of something. Oh sure, the boys bickered and bled each other, but that was just how the Strikers would always be. It was something she and Mila and Blaire had accepted. Days here were spent with her best friend, and her new other best friend, Mila, who had already grown incredibly important to her. Partly because she took care of Blaire emotionally in a way

Ashlyn loved. And partly because Mila was one of those steady souls who made Ashlyn want to be a better person just by being around her. Ashlyn's relationship with Roman and Gentry had grown as well, and they treated her like a sister now. She loved it. She could always give them shit and know they would dish it right back. They made her laugh all the time.

Asher leaned in and kissed her lips unexpectedly. His mouth softened against hers as he brushed his tongue against the closed seam of her mouth. And then he pushed in against her own tongue. God, she loved the taste and feel of him. A happy shiver trilled up her spine and landed in her shoulders. She shook slightly and smiled against his lips.

Easing back, his blond brows lowered slightly, he asked, "Are you cold?"

She laughed and shook her head, her ponytail tickling her back with the motion. "I haven't been cold since the day you gave me my wolf."

"Sexy," he murmured and bit her neck gently. "Dark." He nipped her earlobe. "Wolf." He kissed her again then clamped his teeth onto her bottom lip before growling that low sexy sound she adored.

ASHER

"Yeah, why didn't you make me a pink one? You made me into your favorite color."

"I told you, my favorite color is blue now."

"I would've been an awesome-looking blue wolf."

Asher leaned back on his locked arms and rolled his head back as he chuckled. God, he was beautiful here in the evening light, his white smile so bright and easy, laugh lines deepening at the corners of his eyes, his muscular neck arched back as he laughed. Leveling her with his silver, dancing eyes, he asked, "Will you never be satisfied, Sparkles?"

"You have it wrong," she whispered, wrapping her arms around his bicep and rubbing her cheek affectionately against the strong curve there. "I'm completely and utterly satisfied."

His voice went serious when he asked, "Yeah? With the pack?"

She nodded.

"With Rangeley?"

Another nod. "Getting warmer on the most important part."

Asher swallowed audibly, and his eyes went completely somber yet hopeful. "With me?"

"*Especially* with you."

When he released his frozen breath, it was slightly shaky, and that smile was back. Her smile. The one he always gave to her and no one else. She felt like the luckiest woman in the whole world.

"I'm the lucky one," he said quietly.

She was used to that part now. Sure, he tried to stay out of her head, but she was thinking loud right now and didn't blame him.

"Are you guys coming or what?" Gentry called.

When Ashlyn twisted around and looked at where the camera had been, someone had already packed it up and Blaire, Gentry, Mila, and Roman were all at the mouth of the trail, staring at them impatiently.

"Bar opens in thirty minutes," Blaire said brightly. "Move your Asherholes."

Ashlyn snorted, and Asher stood gracefully, dusting snow off the seat of his pants with one hand, while offering the other to her.

"Gentlemonster," she said, smiling up at him as she slipped her hand into his.

"Only for you."

"It's true," Roman called. "He's still a boob-dick to everyone else."

Ashlyn giggled as Asher made an irritated ticking sound behind his teeth.

She jumped, clumsily, because apparently being a werewolf hadn't cured the klutz from her—and grabbed onto Asher like a backpack. He rested his hands under the backs of her knees with no protest and began carrying her down the steep trail that led back to Winter's Edge.

"It's not like anyone is going to show up for the Grand Opening," Mila pointed out. "We annihilated the Bone-Rippers, and they would've been our best customers."

"Well, it'll be a private party then," Blaire said optimistically. "We can make grilled cheeses and drink ourselves silly and call it the first official pack meeting."

"If we get one customer in there tonight," Gentry said from up ahead on the trail, "I'll be surprised and will see the grand opening as a success. It's taken us so long to finally get it re-opened."

"I'm kind of proud of us," Mila said from where she had linked her arm with Roman's. "Winter's Edge went under attack time after time, and sure we were mad, but we started clean-up the next day, every time, no complaints—"

"I complained," Roman corrected.

"No complaints but Roman, and we got here, to tonight." Mila sounded so mushy right now, it conjured Ashlyn's own emotions about their journey to this moment.

Thankful, she nuzzled Asher's neck. She had a strong pack. Ashlyn was really proud of them, too.

Up ahead, she could make out the side of Winter's Edge. Gentry and Blaire skidded to a stop at the mouth of the trail so fast Roman ran into the back of them and muttered a curse as he tried to shield Mila from doing the same.

The string of obscenities died in Roman's throat, though, and he stood as frozen as Gentry and Blaire.

"What's going on?" Asher asked, stepping around them.

Ashlyn gasped at what she saw. The parking lot to Winter's Edge was full, and the line to get in stretched around the building. A few of the townies saw them and waved.

"It's cold as balls out here, Strikers," a man in a police uniform called out. "Let us in."

"Holy shit," Asher murmured, scanning the line.

"Holy shit!" he said louder as he got his legs moving.

Ashlyn laughed in shock and held on tighter as Asher began to jog for the back door.

"Move it, fam," he called behind him in that tone that was impossible for any of their pack to ignore. The order brushed across Ashlyn's skin and made her want to obey. Asher was a good alpha, though, and didn't often use his powers of command unless it was important.

As they made it through the back door, Ashlyn turned to see the others jogging in after them, shocked smiles on their faces.

Asher set her down gently in the kitchen and said, "Can you get the food going? Roman and Blaire will help you. Me and Gentry and Mila will take care of the front."

"Okay," she whispered breathlessly. Movement caught her eye, and she called after her mate, "Asher!"

The others were organized chaos around them, rushing to work already, but Asher spun and made his way back to her, kissed her hard. She could feel the excitement wafting from his skin, and it fueled her own. He disengaged with a soft smack, and she whispered, "I just wanted to tell you I'm proud of you. And Happy Grand Opening. And Asher?"

"Yeah?" he asked, searching her eyes with a small smile curving up the corners of his lips.

Ashlyn twitched her head toward the corner near the freezer. Asher's father was there. Odine flanked him, her hand cupped in the crook of his elbow, smiling with deep emotion in her eyes. They were transparent and cast in a blue glow.

Asher gave Ashlyn a quick glance, then pulled her with him, approached the ghosts slowly as the sound of patrons entering the bar sounded from the front room.

"Hey," Asher said low.

His father's face morphed immediately into a smile, and his eyes locked on Asher. "My oldest boy," he said. "I've said my goodbyes to your brothers because your mother and I will be going now." He scanned the kitchen, inhaling deeply as his smile got wider. "I was waiting for this day to come. I wanted to see it before I went."

"The re-opening of Winter's Edge?" Asher asked.

"No," his father murmured. "I wanted to see that you were okay, and happy, and with your mate. And also with your brothers again. You're a good alpha, Asher. You'll be much better than I ever was. I should've seen that all along." His dad shook his head sadly. "I'm sorry."

Asher took a step back like it had been a blow. He cleared his throat and nodded over and over before he finally said, "I forgive you, Dad."

"Good man," his dad said. "I love you, boy."

Asher ran his hand roughly over his hair and ducked his gaze to the tile. It was a few moments before he answered in a thick voice, "Means a lot to hear that. I love you, too. Both of you."

Asher's dad smiled, and Odine waved as tears slipped down her cheeks. "Bye now, my Asher Boy," she whispered. Her voice faded to nothing as the two ghosts disappeared, arm in arm.

Asher turned and crushed Ashlyn to him, and she could feel The Taker rolling from him on the tide of her mate's emotions.

"Shhhh," she said as his breath hitched. Ashlyn gripped the back of his hair and hugged him as tightly as she could to keep him from breaking apart. That was her power now. She could keep The Taker in line when Asher was tired. The dark blue fog poured from him and surrounded them, but it didn't hurt her. It only brushed her skin and then made its way back into Asher. Odine's prediction had been wrong about that. The Taker hadn't been cured from him, but then again, that had never been Ashlyn's intention. Asher had never needed to be fixed. All the parts of him were perfect—Man. The Taker. Dark Wolf.

No, he'd never needed fixing.

He'd just needed someone to help him carry the burden.

"Three chicken finger baskets," Gentry yelled through the swinging door. "And go ahead and grab a couple more bottles of whiskey. Someone just ordered shots for the whole damn bar." There was excitement in his voice, and Asher laughed thickly against Ashlyn's neck.

"We have work to do, Sparkles."

"That we do. Let's slay this Grand Opening, and tonight we can go home, and I'll let you feed me grapes and do dirty stuffs to my bod."

The sadness in Asher's eyes disappeared and was replaced with appreciation. "I really am the luckiest," he murmured, drawing her hand to his lips. "I wouldn't want to be alpha without you here, keeping me steady."

"We're a good team."

"The best team."

She grabbed his butt and squeezed, "The sexiest team."

"God, I love you," he growled, his eyes flashing silver.

Asher leaned down and kissed her roughly, biting her lip at the end and leaving her breathless. He swatted her ass, turned, and made his way toward the door that led to the main room of Winter's Edge.

She watched him leave because she knew what he would do. It was the same thing he did every time he left her, even for a moment. He turned right at the door, a smile on his face, and told her, "I'm still not running. I'll be back."

Ashlyn grinned at the man she loved more than anything and waved, tears filling her eyes, because today had been one of the best, most emotional days of her life. She had everything now.

Friends, family, a home in ten-ten with the man who held her heart. No more fear of commitment or distrust. She'd once thought tying herself to a man would trap her. That it would ensure she was let down, but Asher had shown her something so different.

Love wasn't the cage she'd thought it was.

Love was freedom.

And she knew, without a shadow of a doubt, such potent happiness had been waiting for her here all along, with the Wolves of Winter's Edge.

ASHER

Want more of these characters?

Asher is the third book in a three book standalone series called Wolves of Winter's Edge.

For more of these characters, check out these other books from T. S. Joyce.

Gentry
(Wolves of Winter's Edge, Book 1)

Roman
(Wolves of Winter's Edge, Book 2)

About the Author

T.S. Joyce is devoted to bringing hot shifter romances to readers. Hungry alpha males are her calling card, and the wilder the men, the more she'll make them pour their hearts out. She werebear swears there'll be no swooning heroines in her books. It takes tough-as-nails women to handle her shifters.

Experienced at handling an alpha male of her own, she lives in a tiny town, outside of a tiny city, and devotes her life to writing big stories. Foodie, wolf whisperer, ninja, thief of tiny bottles of awesome smelling hotel shampoo, nap connoisseur, movie fanatic, and zombie slayer, and most of this bio is true.

Bear Shifters? Check

Smoldering Alpha Hotness? Double Check

Sexy Scenes? Fasten up your girdles, ladies and gents, it's gonna to be a wild ride.

For more information on T. S. Joyce's work,
visit her website at
www.tsjoyce.com

Printed in Great Britain
by Amazon